THE
EATER
OF
GODS

THE
EATER
OF
GODS

DAN FRANKLIN

CEMETERY DANCE PUBLICATIONS

Baltimore

❖ 2023 ❖

Cemetery Dance Publications
132B Industry Lane, Unit #7
Forest Hill, MD 21050
www.cemeterydance.com

The characters and events in this book are fictitious.
Any similarity to real persons, living or dead,
is coincidental and not intended by the author.

Trade Paperback Edition

978-1-58767-857-8

Cover Artwork and Design © 2023 by Elderlemon Design
Interior Design © 2023 by Desert Isle Design, LLC

Dedicated to my two girls, Kelsey and Layla
To the mother, the mentor, and the friend
And to all those who remain.

"Did he who made the Lamb make thee?"
—WILLIAM BLAKE

CHAPTER

ONE

I n her letter she called it paradise.

A quaint and quiet desert town living proudly in the grip of the Libyan desert, ancient Berber roots running strong among the sand and stone and rugged flowers. A land so plentiful in silver that a local had given her a necklace with a silver disc on it, free of charge, simply because it was custom for the women to wear them even thousands of years after the mines had run dry. They had greeted her warmly, given her shelter and food.

Nine years had passed since then, and nothing remained. Not as she described it, anyway.

Norman absentmindedly stroked the letter in the pocket of his cargo pants as he surveyed the aftermath of her dream deferred. Where Clara had described vibrance and hardiness, generosity and beauty, he saw only the rubble of senseless violence, hopelessness and decay. Al Tarfuk was a dying village, had a year or two left in it, he guessed.

Maybe only months. She had called it paradise, but Norman knew the word that he would have chosen.

Lost.

The journey to eastern Libya took him nearly six thousand miles. From North Carolina to Cairo, then a bus ride to Bahariya, a second bus to the Siwa Oasis, and two days ride on the back of a stinking, surly camel until he arrived here, at the tiny village of Al Tarfuk, roughly sixty miles west of nowhere. At no point along the way did Norman really understand why he agreed to come.

Oh, it made sense on paper. The funding was going through its last spurt in reaction to Clara's death, and there was little to show for their ten years of research. Egyptology was just about as dead as its subjects, as far as the University was concerned. The program would probably not outlast the village. There would be no further expeditions.

Why they chose Norman still confused him, but he supposed he should be grateful. He wasn't.

It should have been Clara.

Clara had spearheaded the entire research into finding the lost queen Kiya, had spent years meticulously poring over half-defaced inscriptions, raising funds, keeping the magic alive in Norman and in everyone else she could infect with her enthusiasm. Clara, who was reduced year after year into a mumbling skeleton by the chemotherapy. Who left him alone on the sunset side of middle-aged, too young to simply die and too old to start over.

She had been insistent that he go and finish her work. History, she said, is what makes the future. Nothing ever really dies if it's remembered.

Norman saw no evidence to support her.

As best he could tell, the majority of the buildings that still stood were dottering, bomb-scarred hulks near collapse, and most residents lived in a cluttered tent slum guarded by tangled barb wire and the occasional teenager toting an assault rifle. Norman could smell the stink of sweat and sweltering rot and abandoned waste so strongly that it left a taste. He couldn't help but notice there were very few adult men.

They'd pulled her out emergently the same night she wrote the letter. Gaddafi had been dragged through the streets of Sirte, shot in the stomach, raped and tortured and God only knew what else, although Norman suspected God wisely kept His distance. Civil war swept across the Libyan countryside in a volcanic wave of blood and bullets. Militias formed, petty despots rose up and dropped by the day. Everyone wanted someone to blame, persecute, kill, and there weren't nearly enough alternatives to keep the tiny native villages safe.

He should have felt pity. He mostly felt jet-lagged.

Norman picked his way across the sand-studded rubble and garbage, down what marginally qualified as a street, looking for someone who might answer questions.

"Where should we go?" Norman asked.

The woman standing next to him gave an indelicate shrug and fanned herself with a hand. The heat from the sun was unrepentant, dizzying.

"Your call. I'm a fly on the wall," Anita said. "You just tell me what you need to say. But the best way to go about it is to find the oldest man you can and ask him for Hazred. Village this size can't have more than a hundred people. Shouldn't be too hard to find him."

Anita Sidhu was a translator. Forty some years old and sharp-witted, sharp-faced, and sharp-tongued. She wore pant suits to work, but not in funky colors. While she had no particular affiliation with Islam, she kept her head covered and out of the sun. She was one of the few people Norman had met who could speak Siwi as well as read ancient hieroglyphics from most of old Mesopotamia as well as ancient Egypt. Her face was pinched and her eyebrows seemed

forever furrowed in concentration and when the Egyptology program died, he had no doubt she'd do alright.

Norman eyed the tent hovels. The oldest man he could see
watched the two of them under the shadows of a tent made from
layered dingy carpets. His beard was a patchwork of crusted filth
and his fingers dug into a young girl's bony arm just below the knob
of her shoulder. She couldn't have been much older than ten, her
face bruised and hollow and completely disinterested. She did not
struggle when he shoved her back inside and slunk in after her.

The University had reliable reports that Hazred was still alive,
but no one had managed to reach him directly. Not since Clara had,
nearly a decade before. If they couldn't find him, they would go person
to person, interviewing, to see who else might know what he knew.

The thought was a hopeless and overwhelming one.

A boy loitered at the slum's metal link gate, his face a mess of
scars that led up and across one cheek. The eye above them was
milky and blank. He looked twelve or thirteen and dressed in mot-
tled rags. His good eye fixed on them as they approached and he did
not step out of the way.

When Norman tried to step around him, the boy shouldered his
way back in front. He held out a hand, palm up.

Norman looked at Anita.

"Can you tell him to fuck off? But gently."

Anita cleared her throat and warbled out something in Siwi. She
didn't seem too interested in the part about "gently."

The boy shook his head, jabbered wildly in the curious, local
dialect. He poked at Norman with one long, dirty finger.

"Anita?"

"He says he was waiting for us. Hazred said there were Americans
on their way. Guess that makes our day easier, huh?"

The boy turned and scurried off through the tents. He did not
look back to see if they followed.

The smells only grew worse as Norman and Anita waded through the slums. The yellow-brown stench of body odors, of raw meat spoiling in the hellish heat, of garbage and feces. The deeper they went, the greater the disrepair. Norman wondered, for a moment, if they were about to get robbed or murdered.

The boy waited by the mouth of a marginally cleaner Bedouin tent, his foot tapping in impatience. He cocked his head toward the opening and held out his hand.

"Nope," Anita said. "Don't give him anything. Not here. Maybe later."

He did not lower his hand as they passed by him and leaned to look inside the tattered tent.

Norman squinted, let his eyes adjust after the branding sear of the sunlight. It was cooler inside, darker. The tent was a mess of linens and the charred carcasses of furniture but the floor was mostly clear. A man sat on a ragged rug that was a bored, weary shade of beige. He was gaunt and spidery, his face as inhospitable as the land in which he lived. His smock-like jellabiya was tattered, the color of bone. A tea kettle steamed merrily on a portable stove hooked up to a grunting generator as he crushed a small collection of leaves in a pestle.

"Excuse me," Norman said. "This boy brought us here. We're looking for Hazred. Have you seen this man?"

Norman fished around in his pocket for the polaroid he kept next to Clara's letter while Anita translated, her voice navigating the twisting vowels. Norman wished they spoke Egyptian. He wasn't fluent but he would have some idea of what was being said. It wasn't that he didn't trust Anita, but it was disconcerting, having no idea what words were being credited to him in such a grim and angry place.

The man in the picture was obese yet attractive, smiling, with rich, dark hair and a twinkle in his eye to match the smile. Like a brown-skinned Santa Claus, Clara had once joked, her face flushed with guilt at the vague racism. He sat in a high-ceilinged room with his back to an exquisite shelf of polished wood, packed full of porcelain tea sets. It was an old photo of Hazred, but it was the best anyone had. Clara had taken it. Norman handled it as if it were a sacred text.

He held it up for the spider to see.

"His name is Abdullah Hazred. We're looking for him."

"There's little to see," the man responded, before Anita could translate. His English was clipped and precise and unmistakably British.

TWO

"Y ou're Hazred, aren't you?" Norman asked.

He glanced at the picture in his hand for reference. Nothing much linked the spider to the smiling man besides maybe his eyes. Norman marveled at what a difference a decade could make. When he thought of Clara, it didn't seem so impressive. What a difference a year could make. A day.

Hazred nodded slowly, thoughtfully. He dumped the contents of the pestle into the kettle and breathed in the steam as it steeped.

"You've come for Kiya, haven't you?"

The question took Norman off guard. He shared a look with Anita. The woman shook her head, clearly at as much of a loss.

"How did you know?"

Hazred sighed and gestured to the both of them.

"Come inside."

They did. The low ceiling was crisscrossed with knotted rope from which all sorts of things dangled, from laundry to pots and pans. Norman had to duck low to keep his head from clattering into a pair of oil lamps that hung, cold and dark, with coiled wicks as thick as rat tails. His knees popped as he crouched down, Anita beside him.

"I remember her. That woman. She came here many years ago asking questions about the house of Kiya-Aten."

"Her name was Clara. You didn't help her."

"I did not. Your wife?"

He didn't wait to see Norman nod. He unplugged the stove and opened a tiny cabinet. He took one of two tea cups out, cradled it with reverent care and set it upon the ground. In the back of the cabinet, the remains of a third cup, long since reduced to jagged splinters, settled in an angry little pile. Hazred splashed a slop of milk from an unmarked glass jar before shoving it back in the fridge.

"She passed away six months ago. Cancer," Norman said.

The man paused, eased out the second cup and filled it near to brimming. He offered it to Norman, waited until he had taken it with both hands before releasing. Norman raised it to his lips, the thin porcelain stingingly hot against the pads of his fingers. It smelled bitter as blood.

"If she would have stayed and continued her search," he said, "I would have killed her."

Norman coughed on the steam and quickly set the strange smelling tea away from his mouth. Hazred snorted, picked up the cup and sipped it before handing it back. He bared yellowed teeth in a grin.

"You need not worry. If I meant you harm, I would have no point in subterfuge. It would be as simple as telling Rashid out there to cut your throat. No one would stop him. But I still have some decency left in me. This is my home you have entered. You are under my roof. I would not poison you. I would not have poisoned her either, for that matter. She came to me and treated me with courtesy, as a person instead of an obstacle. I would never have wronged her like that. No, I would've found some quicker way."

Norman glanced at Anita. Her brow was furrowed and she eyed Hazred with open uncertainty. Her hands clenched into fists. She shook her head once, but said nothing.

"Why?" Norman asked.

"Why would I have killed her? Because some things should not be found. Or even sought."

"That's not a reason to threaten someone," he said. He tried to keep his voice from wavering. The thought of this strange old man plotting against his wife should have made him angrier, but it was mostly bewildering. No one had ever wanted him dead, as best he could recall. Maybe as an American, but not personally. Certainly no one had made plans to kill him. He had assumed it was the same for Clara as well.

"I did not threaten her. She asked for my help. I did not offer it."

Norman wished he were back outside, away from the taut ropes and their gallows of possessions, from the spidery man and the bitter tea. From the cloying scent of body odor and must that hung, damp and suffocating, around the piled clothing and heaps of waste.

"You won't help us either, then? I assume you heard about the University's offer."

Hazred studied the cup of tea in his hands before responding. The porcelain was printed in blue with a destrier, the colors faded from use until only the mane and head remained, floating above a blur of dashing hooves. The horse's eyes and mouth stretched wide in exertion or anguish. It matched Norman's perfectly, two from the same set, only Hazred's was further faded. Hazred spoke slowly, when he finally did.

"I heard. It was never a question of money. I have one son left. He is a soldier, and every day I wait for the news that I know will one day come. He fights for... whatever cause, but I know what it really is. All of them are the same. A bunch of murderers. Rapists. Criminals. The same that came through here and left all... this. They'll find him and drag him through the streets of some foreign place. He'll be shot or hung for crimes he committed. And he'll deserve it. I know what he is. Both my daughters are gone. My wife was killed during a bombing."

"I'm so sorry—"

"Sorrow doesn't matter. There is no more light left in this world. I would have killed your wife—or you—to protect this place, back then. What is there to protect?"

Norman took a slow, deep breath. The acrid stench of the incense did little to help mask the smell of the place. Outside, distantly, there was a brief rattle of gunfire. The man didn't seem the least bit curious or concerned. Norman felt a brief moment of kinship with Hazred. They were both part of the same none-too-exclusive club of misery. He kept the distaste from his voice.

"Something like this might be the best protection you could offer. Discoveries lead to money. Money leads to safety. Maybe it could keep this all from ever happening again."

Hazred shook his head.

"There is no protection in money. This may sound silly to a westerner, but there are terrible things in this world. As terrible as war and murder. I have been to the House of Kiya-Aten. Not inside, but I've stood before it. There are stories, here, you know. Passed down for generations. I grew up here. I translated those texts that brought you and your wife to me. But I was young and very foolish and I have learned a great deal since then."

"I've read the stories. About Kiya and the oracle of Amun and the gods. You can't believe—" Norman caught himself, but not before the damage was done. Hazred looked as if Norman had slapped him.

"Do not mock me. There is only one God. I believe in Allah and the prophet Muhammed. But the House of Kiya-Aten is also real. And some part of the story is too. The local legends say she sleeps. That she devoured every god she could and waits, dreaming beneath the sands. If you had been to the places I have been and seen what I have seen, you would not say this so… carelessly."

Hazred drained his cup, heedless of the billowing steam. He wiped at the rim with the loose sleeve of his shirt. He eyed the cup in Norman's hands as he tucked his back inside the cabinet. Norman wondered how much of the dark, cloudy contents he was expected to drink before he could hand it back.

"It does not matter now. Maybe it is all…" Hazred waved his hand. "And maybe it is not. It makes no difference. I will help you, because I no longer have a reason not to. Nothing can protect us. Your money will help better than any god ever did. I will bring you there, myself. Tomorrow. As for some curse… let it come. If this thing is real, I hope she starts with Allah."

THREE

"Are you sure?"

"As sure as I can be."

There was a long pause on the other end, a snowstorm of static rippling through the speaker on his computer. There was no video feed, but considering his current remoteness, Norman wasn't surprised. Home was a long, long way away.

He didn't need to see the man anyway. He could picture Jerry sitting, back straight and hair freshly trimmed, at his desk. Jerome Menzer was the director of administration and finance which put him roughly equivalent to God, when it came to the University's use of money. He was almost humble enough to brush the idea away with self-deprecation.

"Well, shit. Did he say where it was?"

"He said he would take us there. Not sure much else would help besides GPS coordinates."

"Good. It might not be completely ransacked then. Holy shit. My man! Clara would be proud."

"Mm."

Norman fought to keep his voice neutral. He was glad for the distance, the remoteness of the village. He'd had to video call his check-in back in Cairo, and trying not to openly grit his teeth on camera was much more difficult.

"How are we gonna get out there to bring it all back? You're talking about a fortune. If it's still there. KV62 was packed full. If Clara was right, there's gonna be that much or more at Kiya's tomb. Possibly a whole lot more."

"I don't know how much is left. He said he's been there before, but that he never entered. His family knows about it, a few other local ones, so there's a good chance of some looting. Only…"

"Only what?"

"He seems to think that the locals are true believers, the ones who know where it is. And he's a true believer, too. He's scared of the place. Thinks it's cursed. He said he was there before and that it hadn't looked ransacked. Not like much Kiya stuff shows up on any black market either."

The audio feed stuttered, the man on the other side distorted into a flipbook of sound.

"What?"

"I said 'God bless the superstitious.' That and that I'm sending armed guards."

Norman shook his head, stared at the stony wall. The cramped stone house was one of the few not obliterated. A carpet hung from a wall, doing its best to hide an invasion of spider web cracks in the stone. Dust stung at his eyes and coated everything, danced acrobatics as it descended from the ceiling in response to a crash from the floor below.

"You don't need to do that."

"I want it documented, protected. I want camera crews, I want live footage, and I don't want to end up with some botched mess after all these years."

"Jerry, we're trying for surgery here, not rape. A whole group of people will bring way too much attention and then the looting will be out of control. You know how much stuff went missing from '55. Besides, we don't really know what we'll find in there. Could be nothing at all."

Norman could almost hear the impatient expression on the director's face. He'd known the man for almost as many years as he'd known Clara. In Jerry's mind, they had already found a treasure trove that would have his name on buildings and on the lips of countless generous benefactors who wanted to be a part of a discovery long after their investment would actually have helped.

"Look, you guys are only six hours ahead. I'll have my phone on me at all times. It's hooked up to this app thing, it'll let me know if you call. You get out there, go inside if you can, look around. Find out what we need, what all we're talking about here. You see anything good at all, you call me and the cavalry will come."

"Will do."

"In the meantime, I'll make a few calls. I'll have one of the firms send you a specialist to help escort you. In case the locals cause you trouble or you have any issues. Civil unrest doesn't seem as bad right now, but you know how these things kick up. Especially with money potentially involved. I'm not taking chances."

"I'd really prefer—

"Norman, your safety is the most important part of it. You and Anita and Ms. Levine. Okay?"

He added the sentiment far too late to seem entirely legitimate, but Norman supposed it was better than nothing. Even if an armed guard was as likely to keep him from getting sticky fingers as anything else. He thought of Hazred's empty yellow grin and the hungry, haunted face of the man gripping the girl's arm. They were all desperate. Desperate people and the prospect of riches were dangerous in combination.

Truth be told, a bit of security might be a good idea.

"Anita, Charlie, and me. Not Cal?"

Jerome snorted.

"Fuck Cal." He could almost hear the other man's smile. "Ah even Cal. Make sure he keeps his hands off Ms. Levine. We're all dinosaurs, that girl is the future."

"Will do."

The voice on the far end stuttered again. It crackled, turning the voice into a distant, stumbling whine.

"…care," Jerry said.

The line went dead.

Norman sat and watched his computer screen for a minute or two, waiting to see if Jerry would call back, but he doubted he would. He knew the man well enough to understand how he functioned. Pleasantries were through, now he would be checking which hired gun he could send that would be thoroughly reliable but still potentially keep the price reasonable. And then when it was quitting time, he would go home and not think about them again until morning.

He was right, though. Norman should be proud. He should be thrilled. This was the discovery of a generation, if it panned out. A realization of Clara's dream. He mostly just felt numb.

He fished out one of the collection of travel-sized bourbons he had stashed inside his bag. He'd gotten them on the plane. Wildly over-priced, but the trip was bankrolled and it wasn't like there'd be much need for funds after the expedition.

Jerry could pretend otherwise, but they both knew this was the last hurrah for the Egyptology program, no matter the outcome. There just wasn't much demand for mummies these days.

He drank half of the bottle in a swallow.

The hot weight of the liquor going down made him feel immediately unsteady. He wasn't much of a drinker, and old dogs took slowly to new tricks, but he sure was giving the habit a try.

He splashed his face with water from the sink and glanced at himself in the mirror. It was hard to look too long. Fifty had come like a freight train. Now nearing sixty, he felt all used up. The old man looked back at him, eyes bleary and bloodshot, face settling into deep creases around the foundation of a steadily more permanent frown. It seemed so recently that he had been firm and smooth and smiling, carrying life so lightly on his shoulders. That she had been there with him to fix his tie and laugh about that first gray hair.

For a moment, he thought he would be alright. For a moment he almost was.

Afterwards, he cleaned the traces of helpless sobbing off of his face and washed down his gout medication with the second half of the bottle. He reset the pill timer, straightened his clothes and hair, and closed the door behind himself as he left.

CHAPTER
FOUR

Spotting his companions was easy.

They were all staying in the shell of a house that had been converted into a makeshift inn, crashing in spare rooms that once housed a wealthy family while the living quarters had been converted into a bar. Norman chose to think the family had moved out voluntarily. The rooms were cheap and the options were limited so he also chose not to think about it too much.

The room below was a dimly lit mess of sullen faces, smoke, and the musical murmur of the local Siwan language that Norman never had been able to pick up. Dust leaked in the open door along with the sunset, permeated and danced in the smoky air in tiny whirlwinds. The air hung heavy with the smell of stale sweat and alcohol. Some things, he supposed, were universal.

Norman waved to the scarred man who slouched in what had once been a kitchen but was now lined with several dented kegs instead of cabinets. The scarred man nodded with only the briefest eye contact. Norman made his way among the mismatched tables to the others.

"Well here's to the man of the hour," Cal said. "Big day tomorrow, huh?"

Norman might have believed it was genuine, but Cal's opinion of him was hardly a mystery. He had worked with the University longer than Norman, had every reason to be placed in charge of the expedition, but after a few questionable complaints from certain female TAs and Clara's deep and abiding dislike of him, he had been all but frozen out from the project. Until her death anyway. Now he sauntered along in his sport jacket and sunglasses with all the careless contentment in the world. As far as Norman was concerned, Jerome was right. Fuck Cal.

Anita and Charlie sat side by side, Anita still in her pantsuit. Charlie wore a Miskatonic University T-shirt. Norman let out a snort. Jerome would give her hell if he found out about that. At the other end of the table, the boy who had led them to Hazred hovered awkwardly next to Cal. The lower lighting helped hide his scars.

"You know it. We leave bright and early. Six sharp. Set an alarm. Have all your gear. What's he doing here?"

"The boy? He's celebrating with us! You're old enough to drink, right? I'll buy you one."

The teen stared at him without comprehension. Cal cleared his throat and fumbled the offer through in Arabic, and the boy began looking hopeful, if no less confused. Anita held up a hand, but Cal waved her away.

"Nevermind. I'm sure he understands," Cal said. He slipped a five dollar bill out of his pocket and slapped it into the teen's open hand. Cal clapped him on the shoulder and steered him toward the kitchen. "Let's get you a drink!"

Charlie snorted as the two careened away.

"Hey, at least there's a language barrier. Should keep him from having to worry about most of Cal's bullshit."

Norman had only known Charlie a few days, but from what he could tell she seemed incapable of keeping her wit to herself. Anita frowned after the two.

"The boy is here because Charlie there gave him a twenty for taking us to Hazred," Anita said. "Feed strays and they come back. Cal better be ready come tomorrow."

Norman wondered if she could smell the bourbon on him.

"His loss if he isn't. Jerry gave the greenlight. We're heading out as soon as Hazred comes by to pick us up, no matter what. Will be an early morning."

The bartender pushed a clay mug in front of Norman, muttered something hopeful in Siwi. The beer inside tasted suspiciously like watered down Bud Light. Or urine.

"Aren't they all?" Charlie asked. She yawned a magnificent yawn against the back of her hand and shivered. "Fucking jetlag. I swear. Or camel lag? Any sort of travel just kills me. I'm tired enough that I actually might manage to sleep. Besides, the sooner to bed, the sooner tomorrow."

Cal collapsed back into his chair. The boy lingered behind him, staring with something close to awe over the brim of a massive mug.

"Pussying out already? Night is young, my friends. We're supposed to be celebrating."

"Isn't it a bit premature to celebrate?" Anita asked.

"If you're not first, you're last."

Cal winked at her.

"You're exhausting."

"You have no idea," he answered. "Charlie, you really going to bed already? Don't want to see what we can scrounge up in the town? Maybe live a little? You're too young to be this boring."

Norman couldn't keep the expression from his face. Cal saw it and his mouth gave a sour twist. He rolled his eyes.

"Fine. You guys have fun doing your thing. I'm celebrating. The boy will drink with me, I bet."

"Dawn," Norman called after him. Cal waved a hand in response as he drifted off toward the bar. Two men yammered away, shaking fingers at each other until the bartender shuffled over to them. Whatever he said reduced their argument to angry mutters and hate-filled glances. A distant rattle of thunder rolled in the distance. It took Norman a moment to realize it was probably gunfire.

Charlie yawned again, even wider. Her jaw made a sound like Norman's back did most mornings, and he winced.

"God. I thought you people were supposed to be old and tired. I'm dying here. I hope I have that much energy when I'm his age. And that I know how to turn it off too." She shook her head, tossed a crumpled up twenty on the table. "Night, you all."

Norman raised a hand, Anita gave her a hug, and then she was gone. Norman watched the heads turn as she left.

The woman was unrelentingly beautiful. It was almost irritating. At 26 she had a PHD in anthropology with a specialty in ancient Egypt and a minor in photography. A small building on campus shared her last name. She had the looks, the pedigree, and the brains. It was rare enough for anyone to manage even one of those. Jerome was right; Charlie really was the future of the University. He couldn't help but feel obsolete.

"I heard your speech," Anita said, once Charlie was gone. "The one about your wife. It was beautiful."

Norman nodded dutifully.

He barely remembered any of it. Most of what he could recall of that awful night was sweating and trying not to stammer, of bright lights and applause. How his voice gave a pubescent crack when he forced himself to say her name. Oh, they all had loved that. The bastards. A blur of handshakes and well-wishing afterwards that made his skin crawl. *She's in a better place. It will get easier. I'm so sorry for your loss. Isn't the generosity of the donations to a cause she loved so inspiring?*

She wasn't. It didn't. They weren't. Mostly it just inspired hateful contempt, when he could muster the energy. He rarely could, anymore. It was easier to nod.

Norman peered into the clay cup. He didn't know what else to say. The bourbon from before smoldered like magma in his gut. It seemed Anita didn't know what to say either because she flushed and shook her head.

"I'm sorry, I didn't mean to… I know you. I took one of your classes, once."

"Oh?"

"Yeah, about ten years back. I was a poetry major back then. I thought with my background in languages I could mend the world's ills with heartfelt words."

She snorted. Norman smiled. He had thought that too, he supposed. He'd loved the subtle density of poetry, how such a sparse collection of words could mean such different things depending on interpretation. He even slummed his way through the Psalms, way back before his faith had turned to ash, and not only out of some sense of religious obligation. Misanthropic kids always seemed to either pick up with worshipping books or loathing them.

"Shakespearean? Please not another Shakespeare fan."

"Contemporary mostly. But I can appreciate the classics. 'In Xanadu did Kubla Khan…'"

"'…and drunk the milk of paradise.' Coleridge was stoned out of his mind when he wrote that, you know."

He took a sip of the beer. The second taste was no better than the first. It was, without a doubt, not what Coleridge had been talking about in that final stanza. Anita nodded.

"Everyone knows that. I heard the tape from Hazred's philology seminar too, even before they chose me for this expedition. I even met Clara once. She was a good one. The whole department is inbred, isn't it?"

"Running out of things to discover, I guess," Norman said.

"One less thing, after tomorrow. You excited?"

"You know it," Norman said.

He watched as the two men started arguing again, louder this time. One stood up and as soon as his stool hit the ground the bartender was back. He had an assault rifle slung loosely over his shoulder this time. His fingers traced the stock beside the trigger and his posture said nothing gentle. The two men slunk out into the street like feral dogs. Norman glanced around, but Cal was nowhere to be seen.

Anita fidgeted. Norman knew she wanted him to give an opening, help some exchange, but he didn't know what to say. He seldom did, anymore.

"Well, I will leave you to it. Dawn tomorrow?" She asked.

He nodded. She took a last sip, stood and drifted off toward the staircase too.

Norman nursed the drink until it was low, until the sun completed its chariot path and slipped, bruised, into the black. He gestured for another, and then another.

He tried to tell himself that it was all already decided. That it might really all work out, but he wasn't even sure what that meant. A name on a building was the same as a pyramid or a pine box. Mortality had no patience for pride.

And yet for all that, his stomach ached with a Christmas Eve sort of wanting. With hope. With an uncomfortable, unpleasant desire that bordered on lust. It was easier than ever to play out the fantasy.

That the history books would remember him alongside Howard Carter, that it would be his discovery, his and Clara's, that brought to light the hidden truth about the lost queen. The interviews, the books, the pride as he lectured. And staring into the bottom of the cup, he knew that whatever they discovered, none of it would help. At the heart of it all, he didn't just want answers. He wanted some reason to keep questioning.

He wanted his wife.

When he left for his room, the chill of night already leaked through the doorway and the crowd was thinning and despite all the similar feels of a bar approaching last call, he couldn't help but feel that he was a very long way from home.

CHAPTER
FIVE

The dune buggy grunted its suffering like a whipped animal, shuddered with spastic effort as it slowed to a halt, but Cal found himself laughing just the same. The night air was bitingly cold but it was only out of habit that Cal clapped and rubbed his hands together. He'd always prided himself on being impervious to the elements.

"Well, how about that? You scrawny little sand sniffer."

He ruffled the hair of the boy sitting beside him. The half blind boy, unsmiling, shrank away from his hand.

Cal hardly noticed.

In front of him, a domed burial mound rose, the size of a small cathedral. In the moonlight the sand looked like bone. Stone constructs hunched around it, but Cal didn't pay them much mind. They weren't why he was here. The mound—it was more of a worn-down Libyan step pyramid than the more architecturally inspiring Egyptian ones—was the reason he had come. It was so eroded that a careless man might have mistaken it for something naturally occurring, but no, one look at it and Cal was convinced.

It was real. The discovery of a career, of a lifetime. Of a whole lot of lifetimes, if it turned out to be what he thought it might. He took a swallow from his flask, the Jameson even warmer in his mouth when contrasted with the razor-edged chill of the night.

"Should have been me, my friend," he told the boy. Cal thought his name was Rashid or Rashee or something like that, but he didn't want to ask at this point and didn't particularly care either.

The boy stared at him without comprehension. Pantomiming the idea of the trip with no translator had been a trial, but once the kid understood he was asking about Kiya, it had come down to a simple negotiation. He considered trying to fumble an explanation in Egyptian, but his brain was blurry from the lukewarm beer and the Jameson and the bitterly cold night. The boy only really knew Siwi anyway. His Egyptian was worse than Cal's.

It really should have been him, too. Clara had been the only one who had put in any similar amount of time, and she had discovered her own tomb instead. It should've been his name that would go on buildings, not fucking sad-eyed Norman's. The miserable old shit would probably name it the Clara building and have her reburied there so he could worship her, never mind that she had barely remembered to play hard to get when Cal grabbed her ass at the faculty Christmas party.

The whole expedition was a bit of a train wreck fueled by pity for Norman and the sunk cost fallacy of investing in Clara. If Cal had been in charge, it would have been different, but his career had been scuttled years ago when that pretty little TA got too wet for him. Daddy issues. Granddaddy issues, if he were being honest. He may have been getting old, but they always stayed the same. Girls these days were wild. He supposed he should thank feminism for that.

Amy was 22 at the time anyway, an adult and old enough. Grad students should be fair game. They kept him on board because of his years of devotion, but no more limelight for Cal, no siree. He wondered if Charlie thought about him when she rubbed herself. From the way she chattered at him, he was pretty sure she did. Other names and pretty faces came to him but he pushed them aside. He thought he might've had enough to drink, so he tossed the flask on the seat as he climbed out. No sense getting sloshed or maudlin tonight.

Jerome could plan what he wanted but Norman wasn't going to be the first one inside, and neither was Charlie.

Neither was Cal, he realized. The door to the tomb was open.

Fuck.

"You been in there?"

He gestured at the door. The boy shook his head in urgent denial.

"Well, today's your lucky day. Mine too."

The black slit of the doorway was big enough to let them inside, but it didn't look wide enough for looters to have dragged anything impressive through. There had been gold-plated coffins weighing hundreds of pounds at Tut's tomb. There was no way anything of that magnitude could have been slipped out. Assuming Kiya had managed to make off with as much wealth as the rumors said. Cal clapped his hands and scrubbed them together. He'd know soon enough.

"Come on, you're going in too. Can't have you bugging out on me."

The boy shook his head again.

"What, you afraid of mummies?" He thrust his arms out, stared blankly ahead. "'Im-hoteeeep.' No? I guess that doesn't mean anything to you. Pretty sure you guys never got drive-ins in this hellhole. Poor bastards. Alright," he said. "Here."

He slipped a twenty dollar bill out of his pocket and held it up. The kid's good eye followed it, his head cocked to the side and swaying like a charmed snake. Cal rolled the twenty into a ball and tossed it in the doorway.

The kid watched him for a long moment, then peered past him into the tomb. In the sunset of the dune buggy's headlights, the scars on his face looked like silver writing. Slowly, very slowly, he turned back to Cal and nodded. He took one grudging step forward, and then another. Cal slipped by him once he was sure the boy wasn't going to run away and abandon him for Norman and the others to find tomorrow.

The doorway was a tight fit, but Cal made his way inside just the same, into the utter blackness of a chamber that had not seen direct sunlight since back when Europe was still rutting tribesmen bashing at each other with stone axes. If ever.

Cal flipped on the flashlight and Rashid huddled close behind.

The tomb was fairly typical as tombs went. High ceiling, pillars, hieroglyphics all over the place, recounting… whatever. At the far end, a staircase had been cut into the floor, leading down, presumably to the actual burial chambers.

Cal inspected the glyphs and frowned in distaste.

The writing was atrocious. Whatever scribe had inscribed them was about as competent as a dead cat. He didn't bother trying to fumble through the haphazard scrawl. That would come later, when the team arrived and they had time to film everything and pore over it. Make Anita earn her keep. Most of it was just Kiya's name, written again and again anyway. How the ancient dead loved to see their names in writing. As if it made them any less dead.

Instead he scanned across it for keywords. One in particular. He found it a short way down the cramped confines of the staircase, where the path branched off in two directions.

Treasure.

"The treasure of Kiya-Aten," he read out loud.

Behind him, the boy muttered something unintelligible and nervous. Cal passed him the flashlight and leaned in to study the writing.

Rewards, technically, he supposed. Not quite the glyph for trea-sury or even the scepter meaning treasure, but certainly things of value. Let Anita worry about that distinction. It looked a bit like half of a statement too, but Cal wasn't all that concerned. He gestured and the boy followed down the ugly stone passageway. Whatever funds had financed the effort to pave the upper floors had sure been skimped on down below.

That was the problem, in a nutshell. Norman was a timid thing and Anita was a neurotic mess and Jerry was a whore. They spent their time worrying about details and politics instead of pushing forward. They'd sat on a lead to the tomb of Kiya for ten whole years while Clara and the Egyptology program both sick-ened and died, all out of fear and obligation. It left Cal sneaking through a forgotten tomb like a thief, the only one who actually wanted to get things done. Not that he particularly minded. It had a sort of roguishness that was at least as good as Amy's mouth had ever been.

Click.

He felt it moreso than heard it, a deliberate shift in the stone beneath his foot as a lever settled into place. It took him a moment to understand what he was feeling, and then his irritation about Amy and Norman and the expedition and the future of the Egyptology program were blown away and he was shaking, heart pounding in his chest, hands gripping his knees.

Thoughts of automated crossbows and whistling blades slicing down flickered through his head, as much a product of old Indiana Jones movies as any research.

"Christ," he said.

Of course, the traps never really worked. Machines didn't sit unsupervised for three thousand years and still operate. Even so…

Cal took a long, slow breath in and let it whistle out through his bared teeth.

Christ. Maybe, he decided, it was better to wait for the others after all. The trigger plate had worked, and that alone was enough to tell him what he really had wanted to know: the place was not looted.

He turned back to the boy and held up a hand. No sense in letting some local kid get his ticket punched on the off chance some traps had withstood the test of time. No one had gotten hurt and he'd been the first of the crew to enter the tomb. That was his due. It would have to be enough.

Cal eased his foot up on the trigger plate and then he was on the ground, dizzy and confused, the crunch of breaking stone and a hollow boom echoing and reechoing down the ancient corridors, bounding and returning like a distant whisper.

It didn't hurt. Not for that first moment.

The impact was so stunning that he felt nothing at all besides the ground pressed against his cheek and a strange tugging refusal when he tried to bring his right hand to his head. It wasn't until he tried to push himself up onto all fours that he really understood, and then he was sputtering, flailing with the one arm not trapped. He wanted to scream, tried to, but his lungs would not fill. An impossible weight pressed at the back of his throat and in his head, spilled out of his mouth in a slippery mess of blood. He clawed and twisted to look up behind him, choking, sputtering in the crazily bouncing light from the boy's flashlight. His back put up no resistance at all. All he saw was a stone. Fingers of agony laced up his chest and neck but below that… nothing.

The crunch he had heard wasn't breaking stone. His spine. His hips. His right wrist was caught beneath it too, and that was probably what hurt the most, a searing, throbbing fork of lightning that blurred his vision and left him panting around the blood.

With the one hand that could move he groped at the stone slab that had sluiced down, but of course there was nothing for him to grip. No way to leverage or pull himself free.

"Help me!" he gurgled, turning back to the boy. The words fell apart half formed. "Mother of God…" he tried, but it only came out a jumbled mess of wet, broken consonants.

The sound seemed to free the kid from his shock. Eyes comically wide in the dim light, he let out a piercing, terrified shriek and turned to run, not up the steps, but down them, leaving only blackness behind him.

As if he hadn't seen the staircase leading back out at all, Cal dreamily noted. Stranger still, Cal wasn't sure where the staircase leading upward was either.

The screaming continued for a few more moments, fading and eroding until only the echoes remained, rebounding in the sprawling silence of the tomb.

Something popped behind him, a bone imploding under the grinding strain, and the stone shifted slightly.

The pressure became unbearable, his throat filled with something thick and hot and solid and he shook, his hand slapping in uncontrolled spasms against the stone.

His last thought before he expired was that the screams, as they re-echoed and faded away, sounded like a name.

SIX

Norman woke up at 4:30 and stared at the ceiling for a half an hour before washing up in the tiny, cracked sink and visiting the communal bathroom. He shoveled down a fistful of salted peanuts, a pack of crackers and an anonymous, rubbery rope of jerky that mixed with the memory of the bourbon quite gruesomely. He didn't think they'd have a continental breakfast included. He checked and rechecked his backpack, but everything was he same as he'd left it. He buttoned his shirt from the day before and patted at the wrinkles, then he laid back down and stared at the ceiling for another twenty minutes. The clock chirruped to let him know it was 5:45 and time to take his gout pills. He did not bother with a cup of water and they rattled down his throat as he swallowed.

When Norman made his way back down the stairs, he noticed that most of the same crowd still lingered from the night before, their rowdiness replaced with a miserable stupefaction that left them like sunken eyed zombies cringing away from the red light of dawn that wormed in through the open door.

The air was chilly and clear, stirred only by the clacking overhead fan, and Norman was struck, not for the first time, with how strange the desert was. The viciously cold nights, the infernal days. Storms of sand instead of rain, and a sun angry enough that people bundled up to stay cool. None of that back home.

Anita was already waiting at the table, pack beside her, nursing a steaming cup of tea. Her suit looked fresh-pressed. Norman made his way over to her and set his backpack down. It was filled with all sorts of useful things—flashlights, gloves, masks, brushes, writing pads, a tarp—but mostly served to exacerbate back pain that had been hunting him for thirty some years. The real equipment was with the others. The drinks from the night before haunted him like restless ghosts. He had never felt older.

"Sleep well?" Anita asked.

"Hmm," Norman said. "You excited?"

Anita nodded, but cautiously.

"Yes. And no, too. A bit scared. I'll feel better when we see it. If we see it. Not to distrust Hazred, but..." she shrugged.

Norman fought the urge to unzipper his backpack and check through it again. As readily as he had played the fantasy of success the night before, now he found himself running through the fantasy of failure twice as easily. Jerome's disappointment. Cal's scorn. And to head back home and slip into the anonymous hell of a dented mattress in a bed meant for two.

He pushed the thoughts away. Everything Clara knew indicated they were on track. Her name left a bitterness in place of the anxiety.

"Friend of yours?" Anita asked.

Norman looked up. A military man stood beside him, towered really, hard-eyed and bulky and heavily bearded. He wore a strained tan shirt strapped over with utility belts and the pockets of his pants looked packed full. On his hip he carried a holstered gun, and after Norman noticed that, he had a hard time noticing much else.

"Mr. Haas?" the man asked with a polite smile that did not reach his eyes. He held out a calloused hand. "William Sieber. I work for Cetra Security Contracting. Jerome Menzer sent me as security detail."

"Oh, uh, thanks. You made good time," Norman said. "This is—"

"Anita Sidhu. And I'm expecting two more."

His hand shake was firm but not particularly aggressive. Norman had that old high school impression that he was being measured and the results were not in his favor.

"One more," said Charlie, dropping down into a seat next to Anita. Her eyes were puffy and a vest was balled up in her fist, a sunhat strapped over her shoulders. She was still wearing her T-shirt. "Jerry sent us a bodyguard?"

Anita eyed him.

"Lucky us. You won't get in the way, later," Anita informed him. "You know why we're here?"

"The specifics? No. I came here very quickly and the briefing was... not exhaustive. I think they wanted to keep me from getting chatty while en route. I'm supposed to escort you to and from an unspecified location. Excavation may be involved, from the equipment they let me sign out."

"We're doing something delicate. And we don't need an idiot waving a gun around or trying to steal stuff."

Sieber directed the same polite smile her way.

"Ma'am, my job is to make sure you get where you need to go and back, safe and secure. Nothing more."

Anita shot Norman a look that plainly showed her feelings on that idea. Norman shrugged.

"Not my call," he said. "Director's orders."

"You're built like a refrigerator," Charlie informed him. "God. You ever get to tell people that they won't like you when you're angry?"

She let out a snort.

"Ignore her," Anita said. "We are all just a little nervous."

Sieber shrugged again. The smile was more genuine.

"I suppose that leaves Mr. Calvin Lange. Any of you heard from him?"

Norman checked his watch. 6:03.

"I'll go get him," Norman muttered. A grown man needing an alarm clock to show up to the equivalent of the Olympics. Fucking Cal.

Only, when Norman arrived to check on him, the room was empty.

Just a bed of cold, rumpled linen, his suitcase and his laptop. The duffel bag with his equipment for the expedition hunched in the corner, unopened. The wall above the flat, beaten cot was studded with holes that no one had even made an effort to hide.

No note either.

Norman eyed the holes in the wall. They looked awfully like he imagined of bullet holes. Probably from a long time ago, but that did little to help ease his mind. The whole thing was unsettling. The others might not realize quite how important the expedition was to Cal. Sure, he might pull the rock star routine, but Norman had known him for many years. Asshole or not, like Norman, he lived for this stuff. And even more than that, he lived to make sure he got his due.

Horrible, grisly alternatives poured in. Ideas gleaned from moribund ticking clock television documentaries about sport murders in blood rooms, about abductions and black banners and sobbing, trembling men in hoods whose captors pruned their fingers for proof of ownership.

He licked his lips, took a swallow of water from the canteen strapped to his thigh, and did what he could to evict the thoughts from his mind, to let impatience wash away the thickest stain of guilt. The water had the green, artificial taste of plastic. Cal would be fine. That was all media hysteria, like razor blades in Halloween candy, or men waiting underneath cars to slash your Achilles tendons and carve out your throat when you fell.

If they missed their opportunity with Hazred they might not get another chance. He knew without a doubt what Cal would do if the positions were reversed. He jotted down a quick note and slipped it under the cover of Cal's laptop and left. He took the duffel bag with him. His worries followed like a shadow as he made his way back to the others.

By the time Norman had returned downstairs, Hazred was standing in the doorway, eying Sieber with an impatient sort of distrust and tapping his foot on the ground.

"Not here," Norman said. "I don't know where he is."

Hazred snapped his fingers at Norman and gestured with a toss of his head. He stalked out the doorway, not waiting to see if they followed.

"Told you he'd fuck the dog on this one," Charlie said. "Probably passed out in an alley somewhere. I guess we have to wait for him."

Norman could imagine a few other possibilities. Ugly ideas that reminded him of the girl with the bruised arm and the vacant expression in her eyes as bleak as the shattered buildings. He felt a moment of guilt at his suspicion. Cal had a reputation after that one incident and he certainly was a lot of things—most of them ranging from annoying to directly offensive—but he was probably not that. Probably.

Fuck him, Jerry had said. And joking or otherwise, that was permission enough.

"No," Norman said. "We don't. He knew what he was doing. I'm not going to risk all of this on him. We'll be back tonight and can recon with him then."

It'd serve him right, when they came back in a few hours and found him buzzing around the bar, pissed off and offended. And besides, he couldn't help but remember Clara's look of disgust any time the man's name was mentioned. She wouldn't say why she loathed him, but she did. Seemed a fair enough way to honor her wishes, to leave him behind on the first trip in.

He was fine. Probably.

Anita nodded her agreement. She did not expend much effort hiding a nasty grin.

"That's your call?" Sieber asked.

"That's my call."

"We're really going? God, but I can't wait. We're gonna remember this. Hell, we're gonna be telling this story forever," Charlie said. She pulled her vest up onto her shoulders and her sun hat on.

"You're very into this, aren't you?" the big man asked her.

"If it were a man, we'd be married," she said.

Norman could only think of Clara and silently agree.

CHAPTER
SEVEN

Hazred was waiting for them behind the wheel of a sand-scoured four-door Jeep Wrangler with half-flat tires and a brutally dented fender. Several bullet holes punched pits into the paintless metal panels and the windshield was fanned with cracks.

"Looks like our carriage awaits," Norman said.

"We're getting in that?" Charlie asked.

"We're getting in it."

"The gear?"

Hazred thrust a thumb toward the rear of the vehicle.

"Strap it in," he said. "Tightly."

Only a decade before, they'd have had to load up on a team of camels and forge their way across the barren desolation for days on end. From Norman's recent experience with camels he was willing to allow that progress, however rundown and ugly, still beat the alternative.

Charlie had the decency to keep any further thoughts to herself.
Sieber caught his arm as he headed for the passenger side.

"No, sir. I'm sitting front," the bulky man said.

"Why?"

Sieber looked at him as if he had suggested snorting lines of sand.

"Because your buddy there might not be our buddy. And if he
tries anything—you know, ditch us out in the desert to die—I think
I can at least make sure that he's there with us."

He slipped his sunglasses onto his nose and pulled the door shut
behind him.

"All set back here," Anita called from the back hatch. She patted the meticulously labeled packs of equipment as they perched
among the traction mats and shovels and jack plates that littered
the rear hatch.

Without any more excuses for delays, they began to load in. The
smell of stale air and petroleum pushed against Norman with a near
physical, nauseating force as he climbed into the middle and fished
around for the frayed bit of seatbelt that remained. The cloth of the
seat was rubbed smooth and hard as stone, the torn ragged edges of
sunbaked skin scraping and poking at him as they pulled out and
bounced their way along gritty, invisible paths.

He should have felt nervous, giddy with anticipation, over-
whelmed by the potential that the day might hold. He mostly just
wished Clara were there.

She'd held his hands in her withered, bony fingers, her skin
feverishly hot and papery, and made him promise he would see
it through. That was what he wanted most, just to hold her hand
again. He hoped she would be proud of him. He felt all the more
foolish for hoping.

The sun beat its anger down through the dirty glass as the meager vestiges of civilization fell away and Norman began to sweat
almost immediately. Anita murmured about motion sickness and

sat, eyes squeezed closed as they bounced and jostled over sand. Charlie snored prettily behind over-sized sunglasses as her head bounced against the window. Even her snoring was pretty. He wondered if he had ever been that young. A CB radio crackled up front, but neither men seated up there said anything at all.

And nonetheless Norman couldn't help but stare in wide-eyed wonder at the world outside. The others all had been here before, to Egypt or thereabouts, but Norman had always found some reason to stay home. Clara had been the adventurer, Norman the homebody. They'd had a balance.

He wondered if he'd been wrong all this time.

Rolling crests of yellow baked sand drifted by under the angry, hateful sun. The distant stony ridges simply highlighted the alien serenity of the desert, punctuated by the strange fingers of stone megaliths standing with ancient pride. On several occasions, the tires spun with feverish wanting and Hazred sawed the steering wheel to push them over the dunes, but always at the same creeping pace that felt only a little faster than a jog. The plumes of sand that the tires disturbed hung and tossed in the wind behind them like a restless ghost.

An hour passed, and then another. The Jeep jostled and shuddered but maintained its trundling pace while the sand seethed like cresting whitecaps. Norman took a sip of water from his canteen. It tasted like singed plastic.

Tiny flecks of pebbled glass dotted the sand, catching the sunlight and sparkling like discarded jewelry. Charlie continued snoring. Anita looked simply miserable.

Norman was just beginning to slip into a doze when the sand gave way to rugged graveled stone. Stone pillars and cross beams collected more closely, the pale sand growing redder as it pooled around rocky outcroppings. The Jeep dipped, descended into a cratered depression at a glacial pace and finally ground to a halt.

It took Norman a moment to realize that they had stopped intentionally. It took him a moment longer to see why.

Hazred coughed, cleared his throat, and pointed.

"The House," he said, "of Kiya-Aten."

EIGHT

Norman sat forward, rubbed the grit from his eyes and squinted against the sun. He should have been wearing his sunglasses.

The Jeep had pulled into a sort of natural cul de sac, dotted all over with megaliths, primal in their looming defiance of time and gravity. At the center, a dome hunched, nearly indistinguishable from the surrounding desert. A pair of dune buggies were parked beside it, a cloth lean-to propped up between them. Two men waved from inside the shade and made their way over.

Sieber visibly tensed. Hazred shook his head.

"They are mine. I sent them ahead to make sure we would have no surprises."

Charlie yawned and immediately perked up.

"God but that's magnificent."

Even Anita looked a bit less sickly as she squinted.

"That's it, then?" Sieber asked. His shoulders did not relax.

"Growers and showers," Charlie said around a second yawn. "Egyptian culture was all about the visible size because it's an open desert, but not Libya. This place wasn't always so arid. People out this way built down, not up."

Sieber let out a squawk of protest as Anita pushed open the door and stepped out. Norman followed. The day's heat fell like a hammer, leaving his mouth and hands and nose dry and aching. His joints felt sluggish and even the back of his eyelids purpled when he squinted but he could not keep himself from staring.

This was it. This was why he had come, why Clara had come, the answer to the sprawling mystery of Kiya and the last major piece to a fractured dynasty whose history had been hidden by time and intentional obfuscation.

And the door was open.

He let out a groan.

"Doesn't mean anything," Anita said, joining him. She scraped the sweat from her forehead with her palm. "It's only cracked open. Looters would have left it wide if they had really given it a run over."

Norman nodded. He tried not to wince too badly at the thought.

"This place looks like fu—…it looks like Stonehenge," Sieber said.

He gave a quick, wary once-over of the place before returning his attention to Hazred. Hazred shuffled over to the two men. They babbled in the native tongue, pointed at one of the dune buggies and waved at the tomb. They sounded troubled, but everything in the local language sounded that way to Norman.

It certainly did look like Stonehenge, Norman noted.

A series of stone trilithons the size of stacked buses were rooted in the sand and formed a perimeter around the tomb, their massive crossbars ponderous and unnatural, the shadows they cast forming vaguely sinister writing that swung in a pendulum from every angle around the mound. They looked like titanic fingers upthrust toward the sky. The very existence of them seemed absurd to Norman, bordering on impossible. There was no feasible way anyone without a crane should be able to leverage the crossbeams up, and yet there they stood since time immemorial, alone in the back corner of a forgotten desert.

"It's a warning," Anita said. "It means this is a place of slaughter." She tugged open the rear hatch, sprawled Norman's tarp out on the sand, and began unloading the packs. "That's what the glyph for them means, anyway, and how the Egyptians used them. You're the hired muscle. Help."

"Cool," Sieber said. He joined her, still throwing wary looks over to Hazred. The man was arguing with the other two, now.

"Hell yeah it's cool," Charlie said. She fiddled with her camera, turned and panned across the entire basin. She took a few more pictures before affixing it to a tripod and letting it run. It periodically made a slight metallic clicking sound that Norman had always wondered about, in the age of digital photography. "They're the reason we're here. Not specifically, but like... these structures are five, six thousand years old. Maybe older. Entire civilizations, the collections of millennia of social evolution come and gone and with them their secrets. These things were ancient to ancient people. No one really knows why they were made originally."

Anita made an irritated sound.

"No one knows for sure, at least. It's contested. The ancient Egyptians called Libya the land of spirits and avoided it because of things like them. They're something of a mystery. And you know what they say about history. If you don't know it..."

"You're doomed to repeat it?" Sieber suggested.

"No. It means you're really boring at parties," Charlie said. She squatted down on the blanket, fixed her hair, and began rummaging through the backpacks.

Hazred made his way back over.

He pointed at the door.

"Your missing man, he may be in there. They say they found the buggy Rashid took, and a flask. Rashid did not drink. The boy may have brought him here last night. He may still be with him."

"Did they check inside?" Norman asked. He decided not to shatter any of Hazred's illusions on Rashid's sobriety. He had seen Cal's flask often enough.

"We do not go inside. That is your reason for being here. Not ours."

"Right. The curse," Norman said.

"We will wait here for you until dawn tomorrow. After that, we will go, whether you have returned or not." Hazred looked him in the eye, his face unreadable. "We will not come back."

"Understood. Thank you," Norman said. Hazred was welcome to his superstitions and dramatics. Norman never intended to be more than shouting distance away. He peered past Hazred toward the doorway, but the thickness of the shadow was like a wall, hiding those things within.

Anita snapped her fingers and pointed out a line of goggled gas masks she had arranged on the tarp.

"Take your masks," she said. "We have a spare one, and Cal's."

Norman did. The thing was heavy, rubbery, alien. It smelled like the water in his canteen.

"You really think we need them?" Sieber asked. He hefted it in his hand as if to physically weigh its necessity. "The door's already open."

Charlie snorted as she strapped a hairnet across her head.

"Suit yourself. You know the kind of traps people have found in old tombs? That stuff you see in movies, it's not the half of it. Automated crossbows are one thing. I'm talking acid traps, spores. Sometimes you don't even know you've triggered them then a year later you're puking blood. One of the Bahariya tombs had a room full of hematite dust. If you entered, it would kick up and get in your eyes and mouth. Short term it was disorienting. Long term, it could kill you. I'd rather not breathe lungs full of metal dust, personally,"

Charlie said. She tugged the mask over her grin, took a few rasping breaths and gave Norman a thumbs up. "But maybe that's just me. How do I look?"

She looked like a deep-sea diver, or an astronaut, or some kind of bizarre insect, her humanity buried beneath the thick mask. Anita gave a thumbs up in return. Sieber slipped his mask around his neck.

"Alright," Norman said. He couldn't help but feel superfluous as the two women set about their tasks. He really had no place leading the expedition. "Let's get this show on the road. Everyone ready? We'll set up inside, if there's room for it."

"Check it," Charlie said. She beckoned Norman over to the tripod. She swiveled the camera's screen to face him and tapped it. The picture looked like something out of a textbook. The man standing before the mountain, the lone explorer preparing to enter the tomb. It took Norman a moment to recognize his own face. Christ, he felt old.

In the photograph, the opening behind them looked like the black slit of an eye. Standing closer, Norman thought it looked far more like a mouth with lips of stone nearly a foot thick.

It was open only barely far enough to allow entrance, but a corona of sand spilled into the darkness, formed a thin carpeting across ancient flagstone. It may not have been open wide, but it had been open for some time, Norman realized. Two pairs of footprints led inward. None led out.

If Cal was still inside and waiting to lord it over them, there had to be something worth seeing.

Norman felt a heaviness in his throat, but it was hard for him to say why. Something primitive, instinctual was ringing its alarm. The animal heritage that whispered mortal dread at the sight of implacable stone and the nearness of the dead. It made him feel six years old again, holding his breath as his family's old Buick puttered by the cemetery where his grandparents were buried.

"Charlie, you go in first. You get to cross the threshold. Jerry's orders."

Even despite the alien mask he could see her desire, the way she leaned forward, fingers stroking gently across the camera she had once more slung around her neck. She hesitated, cocked her head toward Anita.

"You sure?"

"He's not here. It's your call," Anita said to Norman.

"It is. Go ahead."

"Diamond in the rough, bitches," Charlie said. The gas mask garbled her laugh into a croak. She gave them each a thumbs up and then squeezed through the slit opening and was swallowed into the darkness within.

"After you," he told Anita.

Anita frowned and shook her head.

"You're the reason we're here. These things matter. Go on in."

He nodded.

He gave one last look to the surrounding desert. To Hazred and the two others, standing side by side and watching them, to the sun seared wastelands and their ancient stone monuments.

Then Norman fitted the mask over his face. He had to squint through the thick glass of the goggles as he shuffled forward. It was probably unnecessary, but it paid to be cautious. His breath roared in his ears and his legs trembled. He set one hand against the thick slab doorway, felt the unyielding, ageless weight of the world behind it.

In that moment he understood why he'd come. For this. Not whatever research came of it, or accolades, or understanding. But to stand before the end of a quest, the realization of a purpose. The beginning and conclusion of the dream he'd shared.

He squeezed past the door of stone and stepped inside the tomb.

CHAPTER
NINE

"**I**t's not a tomb," Anita said. Sieber was still grunting as he pressed through the doorway, bag in hand, and already she was panning her red-lensed flashlight over the walls. Her gas mask hung around her neck, ignored, next to her goggles. "It really says 'the house.' Or 'temple,' I guess. Hard to tell if the crossbar is intentional or not. Can't wait to get this all cleaned up and easier to see. The temple house of Kiya who serves Aten."

Norman slipped the mask off his face and set it on the ground beside the LED lightbox that hummed as it cast the chamber in dim relief. It had a muted lens covering to reduce any light damage, but mostly, from what Norman could tell, it kept it from putting out much of any illumination beyond a sickly, sallow glow. The air inside was cool, a welcome reprieve from the merciless heat of the sun and he breathed in the timelessness, the clean smell of fine, settled dust and a memory of incense that he probably just imagined.

"This is…"

But he couldn't think of the words or whom to say them to. The closest he could come was a nameless feeling of absolute wonder, the kind he had always hoped to find in churches or standing before flags. The kind that started wars.

The antechamber was a sprawling hollow dome, braced by pillar after pillar of stone turned the color of bone by time. The ceiling reached high enough for someone twice his size. Upon every inch of ancient rock, hieroglyphics had been etched and filled in with patched and faded dyes.

"It's something, isn't it?" Anita said.

It was more than that. Norman shook his head. A smile spilled onto his face before he could realize how unfamiliar it felt. He wanted to laugh or cry or shout, but instead he simply smiled.

Clara would have loved it. Thinking her name didn't even hurt. Not here, in such a still and forgotten place. He felt closer to her than he had even in the last few years of suffering.

Sieber let out a low whistle.

"Take it the treasure is gone?"

"Won't know until we go down," Charlie said, waving a hand toward a stairwell near the back that plunged downward into darkness. Her voice muffled through the air processor but Norman could still hear her excitement. "Gotta get set up first. We want this all on camera so no one can call us grave robbers. Grave robbing is like prostitution, it's only illegal if you don't film it and distribute it. Then it's academic. Or pornography."

Sieber snorted. He set the pack down beside the light and Charlie began pulling out equipment. He turned to head back for the door but paused instead and approached the wall next to Norman.

"What's it say?" he asked. "All this writing. What is it?"

"I don't know," Norman said. "I can't read it."

"I thought you were the experts?"

"We are. Hieroglyphics aren't that precise. A lot of it comes down to the individual scribe, and these are... amateurish."

They really were amateurish. Norman resisted the urge to run his fingers over the wall. For one, the symbols were clumsily drawn and etched in so deeply that removing them would have been all but impossible. For two, they ranged from simple recognizable phrases—here below the eye of Aten resides Kiya, Kiya the queen is favored by the Aten, so on and so forth—to rambling, broken sentences that made little sense but made Norman feel vaguely uneasy. The symbols he could identify were angry ones.

The swinging mace: to smite. The man with the bleeding head: to die. The knife and block: a place of butchery. Some of them were altogether unfamiliar. And ugly.

"That one there looks like a stick figure cramming the intestines of a headless... dog thing down its throat."

"Yes," Norman said. "It does."

Sieber gave an all-encompassing shrug and then slipped out the doorway. When he squeezed back in, he had Norman's backpack in one hand.

Charlie tugged the mask down off her head and pawed briefly at her hairnet. "Well I'm not going to be the only dumbass wearing a mask. What Mr. Haas means is they look like they were written by a loony. Or several loonies. Don't worry, Anita will be able to muddle through them."

"He said we have just under a full day, so hope she can by then. I'll bring the rest of this stuff in but I'm staying out front with Hazred and his friends. Make sure they don't get any interesting ideas."

Anita shooed him away without turning from the wall.

Charlie's camera let out a red flash.

Norman looked at the pile of tools. The vast majority of it was still outside, but already they had more equipment than the entire King's Valley team had brought when they found Tut. Most of the equipment was redundant anyway. Gone were the days of hammer and torch. Instead they had digital photography and safety lights and protective gear—more for the things they found than for themselves. Norman suspected that when he was younger, it would have seemed excessive. Back then he would have wanted to get his hands dirty in the old ways.

These days it just made sense. Things were delicate, they could and did break. Caution came more naturally, now that he was so much closer with mortality. Red light caused far less damage than white light. Gloves prevented skin oils from eroding priceless things. Let the later teams worry about the logistics of artifact removal, Norman wanted to leave no trace.

Sieber gently set Norman's backpack next to his own ruck. He may have been entirely out of his element, but Norman nodded his appreciation at the care.

"Smile folks," Charlie said. She hoisted up the camera. "We're about to make history."

The door to the outside released a moan of incredible reluctance and slid shut.

CHAPTER

TEN

The four stood in silence for a long moment, marveling at the sealed door. Norman felt his mouth hanging open and closed it. Sieber stepped forward, a gun in his hand.

"Goddamnit," he said. "God fucking damn it."

"What just happened?" Charlie asked.

"That piece of shit just locked us in."

"How?" Norman asked. It was the first thing that came to mind, even before the slow crescendo of panic that began to build inside him at the idea of being buried alive five thousand miles from home in an unknown grave. He swallowed hard. It helped a little. It didn't help much.

"Norman is right. Maybe it…"

Sieber holstered his weapon and dragged his pack over to the entrance. It left a snake-like path through the sand.

"The door that was sitting open long enough for all this sand to wash in, and it just… what, blew closed? This thing had to weigh tons. Minimum. Last I checked they were over at the buggies, they must have had a lever set or something."

Norman stared at the door in disbelief. Not even a crack of sun leaked through. The light box struggled against the weight of shadows, but it was a feeble, desperate fight. It didn't make sense. The level of preparation that would go into setting a trap like that just didn't add up. And yet the door was closed and here he stood in an ancient tomb with two colleagues and one very large, angry man and no way out.

Sieber pulled a brutish, cast iron crowbar out of his pack and began stabbing the iron tongue into the thin crack of the doorway. The metal ground against the stone with an awful, teeth jarring grittiness.

"Please be careful," Norman said before he could stop himself.

"Really? That's your concern right now? If this doesn't work—and I doubt it will—we're getting out the quick and really ugly way."

"How? We're locked in. They locked us in."

It was harder to keep the panic out of his voice this time. Saying the words sent reality plummeting home. How many days until Jerry decided it had gone long enough and sent help? And without Hazred to help them, how likely would any of them find their way to Kiya's tomb? Norman shivered, hard. The air inside had felt refreshing before, in its cool reprieve from the sun's barrage. It now felt uncomfortably chilly, a remnant pocket of the frigid night festering like rot as it leaked up from below.

Sieber gave one final tug on the crowbar and tossed it onto the ground with a hollow clatter that made Norman wince. He pulled out a small box from his backpack and set it on the ground. He flipped open the lid.

"I come prepared. I've got a key."

Inside the box lay a nest of wires, two small black boxes, and four narrow bricks, each in individual waxy wrapping. Norman stared at the small collection. He didn't recognize it specifically, but it didn't take too much ingenuity to guess what it was.

"You're going to… blow up… the door?" Anita asked. She sounded every bit as aghast as Norman felt.

"I'm saying it's the best chance of getting out of here before this Hazred fellow robs us blind and vanishes. Or gets a pack of friends, breaks in, and kills us."

"A bomb?" Anita asked again, a certain shrillness creeping in to her voice.

"A bomb."

Anita visibly shuddered.

"Let me explain something to you. I'll use small words and I'll take questions at the end. Do you know what a bomb is?" She advanced on him, finger stiff as a blade. Sieber took a step back and set his hand on his holster.

"Ma'am—"

"Ma'am isn't an answer. A bomb is expanding gas in a sealed box. Gases expand until the pressure rips the box apart. This is a stone box. We are *in* the bomb. And get your hand off your gun when I'm talking to you or I'll take it from you and have you sit in the corner. Do you understand?"

Sieber let his hand fall to his side.

"I worked three years in EOD, lady. I know what a bomb is. I know the risks. I'm talking controlled demolition. You said these people built downward, so we can head down and get safe. Blowing through a stone wall isn't rocket science. Pack it in, set it up, get safe and blow it. We'll be back in Tarfuk by nightfall and we can come back out here whenever a proper team shows up."

"We *are* the proper team, you… *ape*. There are other options besides blowing ourselves up."

"Stop," Norman said. He turned to Sieber. "Look if we have to try to blow up a bomb to escape, we can… but we've got to try everything else first. Anita is right. We're not at risk right now. And besides, this... this is history. This is important. There's no back up for this, if it's gone, it's gone. Can we just wait and try to find some other way?"

"The longer we wait, the more chance we'll lose our window to get out of here," Sieber said.

"What if Hazred is trying to help us get out right now?" Charlie asked.

Sieber rolled his eyes.

"Oh, I'm sure he'll try his absolute hardest to save us. So, what now? I'm all ears. What are these other options? Any back doors in ancient sealed tombs?" Norman opened his mouth, but no answer came to him. Anita was still glowering. Charlie, for once, had nothing to say. "That's about what I figured. We have whatever supplies you guys brought on your person. So that is... what, some water and some snacks? Whatever else is in the rest of the packs, sitting out front and might as well be in Nashville for all the good it'll do us. Especially when Hazred jacks our shit."

"Just take a breath, let's not be reactive. We can figure this out," Norman said.

He wasn't sure that they could, though. He had been hard pressed to get any sort of reception back in town with his laptop geared to boost the signal. There was no chance of calling for help down here, under the dome of stone. The wireless tower and electronics were still outside, sitting on the tarp and baking in the sun, along with just about all the other vital equipment. Sieber picked the crowbar back up and resumed fighting the door. The metal bit at the stone and rebounded with a dull, heavy clanging that resonated in his chest. The door resumed being utterly unimpressed.

Norman watched his struggles and tried to think of some helpful contribution, but the harder he reached, the more easily any answers eluded him. It reminded him of a first date, struggling to remember the bullet points he had planned out, the lists of interesting and engaging things to help make himself more appealing. The first time he hadn't felt the need was with Clara. He'd never had a problem knowing what to say to her, or at least knowing what she needed to hear. The thought sat like an anchor inside him.

Charlie's camera flashed. The girl seemed unconcerned by the situation, angling her camera at various parts of the walls as she drifted toward the staircase.

Sieber took a break from his efforts, grunting and sweating and pawing frustratedly at the gas mask dangling, noose-like, around his neck.

"It's better if we stick together up here. This is not the time to go wandering."

Charlie shrugged. Norman found her seeming disinterest in the situation more unsettling than Anita's pacing.

"This might be the only time. You get that door open, we're not gonna linger around here. Especially if you have to blow it open. I'm not a gun-slinger or a specimen of massive physical strength. What I do… is this. If there's any chance of damage, I want as many pictures as I can get, so I'm gonna do what I do until you all are ready to do what you do. Who knows, maybe I'll find Cal camped out down there and he can help us."

Sieber shook his head and went back to work. Norman heard him mutter an extremely unsavory assessment as he strained against the massive stone.

"Not far," Norman said. Charlie flashed him a nervous smile. "You shouldn't go anywhere alone."

"I'll go with her," Anita said after only a moment of hesitation. She clenched her fists so hard they trembled as she approached the staircase. The two headed down, slipped beneath the surface of the black.

"Can I help?" Norman asked.

Sieber turned to him.

"Can you? Sure. You can. Will you? I seriously doubt it. Look, I know this all means a lot to you. Hell, you left your man behind back there so you wouldn't get delayed. But what you gotta know is this all... it doesn't give a shit about you. This is just sand and rock out here. If we're not careful, this could end up really bad. For everyone."

Norman wanted to argue it, wanted to shrug off the other man's concern as fear mongering, to dismiss it as over-reaction because disasters only happened to other people. He couldn't. He knew better than that. Bad things did happen. There was no reason. And help from God... well God's intervention was a thing for the young and the foolish and Norman considered himself neither of those. He had stopped waiting for that when he watched his wife die.

From the staircase below, Charlie began screaming.

CHAPTER
ELEVEN

The rewards of Kiya-Aten, began the inscription on the wall.

...are eternal, finished the slab.

It took Norman several seconds to identify what exactly he was looking at.

What remained of Cal did not look remotely human.

When the slab descended it had rolled the man up like a toothpaste tube with the cap kept on, crushed him nearly in half. The protruding portion was swollen and bloated, tongue bulging and eyes black with pooled blood. Grates on either side of him had drained a sizeable portion of the mess away, but the heavier matter remained caked in a pile, spilling down from his mouth where it had found its only exit.

"Jesus Christ," Norman breathed when he was done vomiting.

Charlie sobbed against Anita who stared, pale-faced, at the wreckage. None of them had stepped off the landing.

Norman turned away to catch his breath. A mural stretched from floor to ceiling, crowded with caveman scrawlings of stick figures cavorting and killing with deranged abandon. Their teeth were jagged triangles, their eyes peered relentlessly back, as if enjoying the voyeurism. One figure stood above them and, one by one, slaughtered the revelers. Any neatness of illustration from the floors above had dissolved into haphazard scribbling. He'd thought anything would be better than looking at the corpse, but now he wasn't sure. At least the cool air helped.

"That Calvin?" Sieber asked.

Norman nodded. Someone should check up on him more closely, he supposed, but he wasn't really sure why besides that they always said to in television shows. His pulse was all over the floor.

Fuck Cal. Those were his last words about the man. He should have felt more guilt, but it was mostly just a startled loop carouseling through his brain, churning forward but without progression. And beneath it all, the thought buzzed around that it couldn't have happened to a nicer guy. He did feel a hint of guilt at that.

"Uh-uh," Sieber said, finally. He started back up the staircase.

Everything felt sluggish inside Norman, time flattened— *flattened*—into a crawl. It took Norman too long to realize what Sieber was going to do and even longer before he could manage to look away from the ruin.

"Wait!" he called out. Norman turned to Anita. "You got her? Don't move. Either of you."

He waited for a curt nod from Anita as she comforted a glass-eyed Charlie and then he sucked in as deep a breath as he could manage and started after Sieber. He tried not to think about the smell. From the moment he started, he knew he had no hope of overtaking the man. Sieber had bounded up the staircase without any apparent effort, but Norman struggled over the carved stone steps. His feet slipped and skidded and the cold air dragged at his lungs and he felt a familiar sharpness in his knees and chest. By the time he stumbled out into the entry foyer, he was dizzy and his legs felt bruised and thick with fluid.

"What are you doing?" Norman asked when he had his breath back under control.

As if it was some mystery.

Sieber crouched next to his rucksack. On a small olive square of cloth, he had set a neat bundle of wires and two black plastic boxes that reminded Norman of garage door openers. He was unwrapping the wax paper bricks. Inside each was a rectangular stick of ivory clay. In the gloom, they looked like butter. The tightness in Norman's chest did not abate.

"Sieber—"

Sieber picked up one of the boxes, the one that sported a red plastic trigger switch. He flipped the trigger on and off three times. Each time, a red light winked on the corresponding second box. He put a safety bubble over the trigger and slipped it into the pocket of his cargo pants. He put on a pair of gloves.

"I'm getting us out of here. We'll come back with a full team and tear this place open brick by brick."

"No."

"Norman, my job is to protect you and your crew. History is great. Sure. But dead people will still be dead tomorrow."

Norman felt a curious disbelief, a rejection of what he was watching, as Sieber prepared the tools of his awful trade. It couldn't be real. There had to be a trick. Some pinch to wake the dreamer, a cue that it was all a scam. It made him think of churches, of late-night evangelicals on television raving in their Sinatra voices with sweat-glistened hair and car salesman smiles. *Do you only believe in the human limitations of your eyes? Or do you believe-uh in the power of-uh God?*

A bomb. An actual bomb. It may have been rational, but it was an impossible blasphemy. An affront against him, against time, and most importantly against Clara. He could too easily imagine the man's condescension as he assured him that none of that mattered. Clara would still be dead tomorrow too. History was great. The thought was jagged and twisted in him like a steel hook. He licked the dry shell from his lips.

"What happened to Cal, that must have been an accident."

Sieber paused.

"An accident? He fell down and crushed himself?"

"An old trap. There are sometimes booby traps left in these places. I've never heard of them really working, it's… it's a fluke. This place isn't dangerous if we take our time and just… just think about it."

"All those things your girl Charlie there said. Poison dust, cross-bows. What, you really think it's safe waiting around for rescue in a place full of killing traps?"

Norman felt a moment of hope. At least the man was listening to him.

"Charlie isn't my girl. And she knows too much trivia. She was trying to rattle you, it's not… Sieber, if you set off that bomb, we're gambling everything. Right here and now. We can wait."

"Do you know what happens if we wait? Our supplies are limited. We can ration them, last for a while, but you're talking about a six-hour hike through the desert once we're out of here. Best case scenario. All assuming this Hazred guy doesn't go get a couple freedom fighters and sit out there with high-powered rifles waiting to play target practice. And that's ignoring the fact that there are ancient booby traps in here that have already killed someone. You know I'm right."

"You can't," Norman said. "I'm begging you."

The desperation in his voice sickened him. He could see it in Sieber's face too, a kind of wariness bordering on revulsion, like a man viewing an addict, or something diseased.

"I'm sorry, Mr. Haas. I know how much this means to you. But this isn't your call. I'm not dying down here for some writing or some gold. There'll be other days."

Only there wouldn't, Norman knew. This was it. The summary of Clara's dream, his dream, the purpose that had dragged him through day after day, the promise he'd made to his dying wife. The years spent reading, theorizing, teaching, hoping. He'd never had any affinity for sports or drugs or women or other addictions. Hell, climbing a staircase made him sweat. For as long as he'd remembered, he'd put his time and trust in three gods—Clara, ancient Egypt, and the Christian God all the priests raved about. Only one remained.

Sieber drew a matte, vicious looking knife from a sheath on his hip and gave Norman a long look. Norman wondered if he touched the weapons as a conscious way of asserting authority or if it was just habit. He forced himself to meet the man's eyes instead of looking at the knife or block of explosive—*explosive*—in his hands. Even thinking the word caused a physical sensation, an esophageal burning like the bourbon from the night before.

Sieber brought the blade down and chopped the butter brick in two. Norman felt a twitch somewhere just above his bladder. As the man packed the two lumps against either side of the door frame Norman found his hands gripping the flashlight so tightly that they shook. For a moment he entertained the idea of swinging it into the back of Sieber's head with all the might he could muster, anything to stop him, but even the fantasy felt foolish. There was nothing he could do to prevent it. No words, no actions, nothing. The summary of all he had and all he wanted blasted into dust and all his learning and all his yearning were powerless to prevent it.

It all felt far too familiar.

"Don't do this," Norman whispered. His voice cracked. "Do you know what all this is? What it really is?"

Sieber drew a pair of red-tipped nails out from a bag, scraped them on his pant leg, touched them to the sand and then paused. He closed his eyes, took a deep breath and let it out through grit teeth.

"Stop. I need to concentrate. This stuff is stable, don't get me wrong. Hell, I could light it on fire, shoot it and run it over with my F150 and it should be fine. But if there's stray charge when I put these in, there's always a chance that the blasting caps will go off and we will turn into canned chili. Not chunky either. We'll be smooth. So please, keep your cool."

When he slid the nail into the block, Norman let a breath out he didn't realize he had been holding. Sieber threaded a wire from the nail into the small terminal box and repeated the process on the other block.

He placed the box equidistant between the explosives.

"What if the bomb doesn't work?" Norman asked.

It was the only thing he could think of to say. He choked back something close to a sob. Sieber sighed, pity plain on his face. The lack of animosity only made Norman feel worse. He should be hopeful, he told himself. Survival really should be the priority. Anything else could be salvaged.

He mostly felt impotent.

Sieber flipped a switch on the terminal box and a green light blinked on.

"The door is made of stone, maybe what, limestone? It couldn't have been more than a foot thick, and these, uh, well these should be enough to permanently deal with that. That's why I'm wedging it in the cracks. Once the doorway is blown open, the explosive force should go out through the opening while the back-blast travels down the stairwell and against the walls. It should be dispersed enough that the walls and pillars hold firm and we'll be down far enough that we'll feel it but it won't actually harm us. We can get out of here. We can get home safely. That's my job. Who dares, wins."

Sieber withdrew the trigger box from his pocket. The trigger was still shrouded in a thick plastic bubble, but Sieber held it with a religious sort of reverence.

"We do not want to be here when I hit this. Time to get the others and strap down."

He gestured, herded Norman ahead of him onto the staircase.

When they reached the others, Norman found them waiting with their backs to the grisly scene. Anita's face held the same panic that he felt in himself. Charlie just looked dazed.

Anita looked between the two men and said nothing. She didn't need to. Norman felt the wheels of his mind spinning for purchase.

"This is far enough," Sieber said. He slipped an orange foam pill into one ear, then the other. He dropped to one knee, placed the trigger box on the ground in front of him and gingerly peeled back the plastic bubble.

The trigger looked tiny in his fingers, nothing dangerous. Nothing disastrous at all. Almost silly. Norman squeezed his hands into fists to keep them from shaking. Too late to change. Too late. Too late.

"Brace yourself," the bearded man said. "This will be loud."

He flipped the switch.

CHAPTER
TWELVE

I t was.

The sound of splitting thunder, a rolling crash and then a stinging wave of heat and sand screamed down the stairwell and slammed Norman against the wall. The blast reverberated like a struck gong, a metallic resonance that left his ears ringing.

He gingerly touched the back of his head where it had clipped against the stone. His fingers came away damp. He could taste blood in his mouth. Next to him, Anita was picking herself up from where she'd fallen. Charlie's hair was in a wild tangle and she pawed sand from her eyes.

"What," Sieber said, "the fuck."

It took a moment for Norman to be able to make out the words. He checked his flashlight. Dead.

"Did it work?" Charlie asked.

"The hell is wrong with you?" Anita snarled. "You could have killed us, you…" she garbled out some term that

Norman didn't recognize. He didn't need to know the language to understand the meaning.

Sieber shook his head.

"Something fucked up."

"Guys? We all okay?" Charlie asked.

"We're okay," Norman said.

Norman took a deep breath and let it slowly out. His ribs hurt. The ringing in his ears was fading, but he still felt vaguely nauseated, like he'd been kicked in the groin by someone with a long and illustrious history of kicking people in the groin. He coughed into the fog of dust that hung, half-blinding, around them.

Sieber passed him his flashlight and flipped the light fastened to his vest on. It feebly stabbed at the dust. Norman chanced a look toward Cal's body, to see how he weathered the blast, and a second wave of nausea sledgehammered home.

"We're fucked is what we are. Let's go find out how badly."

The way back up was slower going. Rubble and shattered stone lay in drifts of sand and dust and nameless debris along the sides of the steps, chunks of cracked ceiling, of wounded walls all leaning in toward the intruders. Norman tried to concentrate on each step and not think too much. He still felt like a rung bell, a latent shuddering energy ricocheting inside his body and mind as he dragged himself back upwards toward the surface.

It didn't take long to get there and Norman wished, with each step, that it would take longer. The entrance to the stairwell was half blocked by crumbled stone, but the gap was still wide enough for him to slip up after Sieber to see what their efforts had wrought.

There was a time, as a much younger man, when Norman would have felt a perverse delight at being right, even in the circumstances. Mostly he just wanted to cry. The destruction was magnificent. What had, just minutes before, been a near-perfect snapshot of an eternity ago, preserved and protected against entropic obliteration, had been extinguished. As if the years had caught up with it all at once, in one fell swoop of heat and force and fury.

The ceiling sagged in toward the hazy fog of disturbed dust that shrouded and muffled the flashlight beams. Pillars leaned against each other, slumped like rootless trees. No sunlight leaked in.

The doorway remained closed. Cracked and seared and cratered, an alien landscape after a meteor cataclysm, but closed.

Sieber shook his head.

"That doesn't make sense. It's a few inches of stone. I used enough that it should be dust."

Most of the room was. The artwork, the writing, they had all been erased or reduced to patchy, muted colors in the shadows of the pillars, like silhouettes of men cast on buildings in the aftermath of an atomic detonation. Only the simplest of the hieroglyphics remained as clear as before, embossed at various haphazard locations across the walls, but they were scorched an angry black and pressed against fractured stone.

Her name. Kiya-Aten.

The devastation left Norman dizzy, nauseated, far more so than the actual blast. He stepped over to the nearest set of runes. He supposed it didn't matter if he touched them now. Preservation was no longer an option.

The hieroglyphic sizzled like a griddle when his fingers brushed it and he snatched his hand away. He bit back a curse. It was blistering even before he managed to unscrew his canteen and dip it inside.

"Metal," Charlie said. "They reinforced some of the pyramids with metals. Copper maybe. Whatever they could find and afford. And, uh, she could afford."

Metal. He groaned.

"Fuck," Sieber said. He turned to Norman. "You didn't think to tell me this?"

"I didn't know."

"You're the goddamn experts!"

Metal.

It made sense. Sieber had said the explosion would blow an opening through the stone door but it hadn't. And when the force of the explosion hadn't been able to divert outward… Norman touched the tender spot on the back of his head. The swollen softness of his scalp reminded him of over ripe fruit. At least it didn't seem serious, no more so than his burned finger or bitten tongue.

"You are the… expert… who set off a bomb in here," Anita said. "Don't blame him for not knowing the structural design of a building no one has entered in three thousand years. I told you it was a bad idea."

"Lady—"

"I'm not a lady. I'm a professional. And please, please try not to… *screw* anything else up."

She trembled with fury. Norman tried to feel it too, but fought a sudden urge to laugh instead.

"You know, we're pretty shitty at being explorers," he said.

The others stared at him and then Charlie let out a snort of laughter. Anita looked a little guilty. Even Sieber managed a grudging smile.

"It doesn't matter now. We can figure this all out. I'd say we head back to the landing where we're less likely to get killed by falling rock. We'll make a plan, see if we can crowbar our way out or something. That sound fair?" he turned to Norman.

Norman wondered, briefly, why the others still treated him like he was in charge. He nodded. There weren't all that many alternatives.

At the landing, they all measured out their water. Norman and Anita were still mostly full, Sieber and Charlie were both half empty.

Sieber sloshed the bottle in his hand back and forth, disappointment plain on his face.

"That's enough to last us a day, maybe two. Water is the big risk. If anyone has to take a piss, keep a bottle nearby. We may just need it. We could be down here a little while."

Norman considered the advice, and whether or not there was ever a point where he would choose to drink the urine of any of the other expedition team. He thought there might be. He hoped there was not. The good humor was fading almost as quickly as it had come. He fought an ugly desire to check back on Cal, to see if the man was still grinning that hideous faceless grin.

"Well, that's just awful," Charlie said.

A distant moaning wail crawled up to them from down in the dark below.

Norman whipped around, aimed his flashlight downward, but the staircase curved, swallowed the beam. The insane scribblings that marred the walls caught the light and in the periphery of the beam it almost seemed like they moved. Under the direct focus of the reddened light, they returned to stone. Reality felt solid again too, immoveable. The feeling of merriment was entirely gone.

Sieber stepped by him, gun raised and aimed.

"Hello?" he called out.

The echo ricocheted, broke into chattering whispers before returning. The cry sounded again, in distant answer.

"Hazred said there was a boy down here too," Charlie said. "The one who went with Cal. It's gotta be him. He's not speaking Egyptian though. At least I don't think he is."

"It's not Siwi either," Anita said. "Not proper Siwi anyway. Not proper anything. It sounds more.... Hurrian?"

"What is he saying?"

They all turned to Anita.

Anita chewed her lip. Her hands were clasped in front of her and Norman realized it was probably the first time he had seen her look anything other than confident.

"The accent is strange, and I don't know Hurrian very well, but it sounds like he's calling out for God. And begging for him to come deeper."

CHAPTER
THIRTEEN

"We have to go get him," Charlie said.

Sieber shook his head.

"We're not a rescue team. This whole thing has gone tits. We need to see about digging our way through and getting back to Tarfuk. Preferably before a handful of Hadjis show up with rifles and drop us as we climb out. He'll be fine for a couple days."

"Down here? In the dark, for days. Would you really be fine?" Charlie asked.

"If we split up—"

"I'm not saying we split up. I'm saying that we all need to go get him."

"What about traps? Your pal didn't do so well playing Tomb Raider."

"That boy is still alive. If we leave him down there, we might as well have murdered him. We'll be careful."

Sieber shook his head again, more slowly. He turned his efforts to Norman.

"He isn't one of us. If he dies… fuck, this isn't smart. You know this isn't smart. You wanted to help? This is how you help."

Charlie turned to Norman too. She must have read his reservations on his face because she didn't bother waiting for him to weigh in.

"Well I am one of us. And I'm not killing some helpless kid."

She hitched her camera bag up over her shoulder and headed down the staircase.

"Come on, are we really…?"

Norman nodded slowly. He felt an angry flicker of joy at Sieber's helplessness after the failed bombing attempt, but it didn't last. It didn't matter, either. Whatever chance he had of dissuading Charlie had passed the moment he let her build momentum for her moral indignation. And she was right, too. A good person would do what they could to save some helpless soul from dying alone in endless darkness. Clara would. That was enough for Norman.

Sieber shook his head in disbelief then headed after her.

"Wait up," he called.

The depths consumed his command and returned nothing. A moment later, even the distant glow of flashlights had vanished as completely as if they'd been submerged in tar.

Anita hesitated, audibly swallowed. She closed her eyes and took a few deep breaths.

"You going to be okay?" Norman asked.

She looked pale.

"I'm not too good in really tight spaces. Or risking what happened to Cal. But hell, if those two can, I can," she said.

"I'll go first," Norman offered, regretting it even before he said it. She nodded her gratitude.

Before he could come up with reasons to hesitate, he turned to face the roughhewn steps. He crossed on to them and began his descent.

The feeling of being digested was undeniable.

The staircase was steep, cramped, and winding as it drilled down into the Earth and with each step it grew colder and colder. Like the oceanic layers, he thought. Down from the sunlight zone into mesopelagic twilight. Down toward the abyss.

The vaulting ceiling of the entry chamber did not carry over and Norman had to stoop to keep from scuffing his head on the ancient stone. The walls on either side inched closer and closer until the runes nearly brushed up against him, the same deranged and violent hieroglyphics from before stretching in one, tireless band at head level. Mostly it just said a name, her name, again and again.

Kiya-Aten.

Behind him, Anita shuffled along. Ahead of him, he could see trace glimmers of the others' flashlights as little by little they closed the gap. He did not let himself slow down. Time melted into a strange blur of footstep cadence, the echoes of Charlie's voice and an occasional wail of dread filtering up from below.

Sometime during the hike, Norman realized his breath had begun to fog. He tried to remind himself that it was hellishly hot outside the tomb, but that did little to help him, so deep below ground and away from the sun. Each step brought him deeper. Each step he grew colder.

And then the staircase finished its course and Norman spilled out behind the other two as they stood in the doorway of a shadow-haunted room.

In the center of the room sat a sarcophagus.

"Holy shit," Sieber said. "Is that gold?"

"Probably just plated," Norman said, but he honestly wasn't sure.

Sieber let out a low whistle. Charlie's camera gave a dull flash. She shrugged, face guilty.

"We'll find the boy," she said. She made no effort to move.

The sarcophagus was a magnificent, gleaming thing that caught the light and painted the wall in an otherworldly metallic glare. Pure gold or not, it was resplendent. Absurdly so, to exist, forgotten, in such a place of darkness. The lid lay beside it like a gigantic ingot. Norman stepped forward to peek inside, but aside from a folded heap of yellowed burial linen, it was empty. The inside was gilt too, etched in a maze of senseless whorls and lines. A common defense in the inner layers of coffins, to keep spirits from slipping in or out. Utterly magnificent.

"Why would anyone build a coffin out of gold?

"If you're going to spend eternity somewhere, you choose it carefully," Norman said.

It wasn't just that, though. He'd seen Akhenaten's coffin and despite being half looted it was a staggering display of beaten gold and intricate detailing. A masterpiece of craftmanship, sure, but nothing on the sheer brutal value of the sarcophagus here. Even the mummiform coffins of Tutankhamun himself were trivial, if more expertly designed. This display of wealth was brazen, staggering. He fought the urge to run his hands over the cold metal. Skin oils could etch metal, given time.

This wasn't built for Kiya. It wasn't even built for her husband Akhenaten, one of the wealthiest pharaohs ever to live.

"It's built out of gold," Anita said, "because it is a coffin for a god."

She pointed at the brief inscription molded into its surface. A circle. The symbol for the one God, Aten. Norman knew too well the thoughts on being buried with a loved one to find it so surprising that Kiya had hoped to share a tomb with her God.

Charlie took another picture. Her look of guilt had faded, replaced by excitement.

"This is incredible! Anita is right. See, the gods were said to have bodies of silver and gold and gemstones. The only fitting resting place for them would be... well, something like this."

Norman wiped at his nose. The coffin was empty, sure, but it definitely had a smell to it, sharp and potent and fairly awful. Like battery acid, alkaline and hair-raisingly foul. Which, he supposed, was peculiar. Any smell should have exhausted itself after so many thousands of years. If there were contaminations, it would endanger any likelihood of finding Kiya's body intact. At least, he realized, grave robbers really hadn't made it this far.

"If it were a pharaoh, it'd probably be occupied. And honestly there'd likely be a bunch of corpses thrown around here. See, the pharaohs invested a lot of their lives into building their own tombs. Sort of a long-term investment. Only, when they did a really good job, the following pharaohs had a habit of dragging the old ones out and tossing them so they could steal the tombs for themselves."

"Not here though?" Sieber asked.

Charlie tucked her hair back behind her ear and leaned in for another picture before answering.

"This is different. People treated the pharaohs as gods while they were alive, but once they died, the belief went with them. This was built for a real God."

"A real God."

Norman cleared his throat.

"What you have to understand is that religion was everything, back then. The pyramids weren't just built by slaves. People fought for the privilege to work there. It was an honor. And rightfully so. They prayed and it *worked*."

"You believe this bullshit?" Sieber asked, eying him up and down.

"No, but they did. The gods controlled everything. They chose the pharaohs, they controlled the weather, they protected the after-life. They spoke to people, they sent visions, they could sometimes even tinker with time and space. People bartered with them, begged them, threatened them. They dominated every facet of life. Kiya and her husband took some efforts to change that, but even they believed in the burial rituals. I do think it odd that there's no inner mummiform coffin though. Usually these coffins come in layers, one inside the next, to help ensure security and to help the dead prepare for the afterlife."

"Wild. I'm a good Christian boy, my world is a whole lot simpler."

"Then your God is another name for Aten," Norman said. "A jealous God who keeps his distance and demands worship and then when you need him…" he shrugged. The bitterness in his voice left a bad taste in his mouth. "Egypt and Israel were neighbors. There's an overlap. Think of this as an Egyptian Ark of the Covenant."

Anita took a sharp breath then let it spill out in a rush. She did not look up from the grate that outlined the base of the sarcophagus. Her brow was sweaty and face pale. "Do any of you…?" She trailed off, shook her head. "Nevermind."

Sieber opened his mouth as if to respond, but then seemed to think better of it.

Norman was grateful. There was a comfort to falling back into his role as a lecturer, but sometimes it just made him feel like he was spitting poison.

The other man dropped to a crouch as he set up the lightbox and the room flooded with sallow semi-light. Besides the coffin and a work table on the far side of it, there wasn't much to see. It measured probably two dozen paces in any direction, the walls crude and uneven, with a ceiling just barely high enough for standing. Even so, digging it out must have been a massive undertaking. Including the stairs, it was bigger than Tut's had been, and that was a rush job that took nearly a decade. Norman wondered, briefly, how Kiya had been able to afford to build the tomb. And all in secret. The scribes alone, no matter how incompetent, would have had to put in hundreds of hours of work.

Alongside the doorway they had entered, a series of entrances stood in an orderly line. Each either led to passageways branching off out of sight or stairwells turning downward. Norman wondered just how deep the place really went.

"So, if this isn't your burial room, this is your treasure room? Shouldn't there be more... treasure?"

Charlie laughed.

"Nope. Neither. 'Treasure room' is a bit of a false name for our interests, though," she said. "Everything from their time is valuable. But yes, the treasury is where they kept the most valuable stuff, and yeah, they packed those full. Furniture. Canopic jars full of viscera. You name it."

"Pardon?"

"Viscera. You know. The wet stuff. Can't leave those lying around. They put them in ivory containers, to keep the remains of your humanity intact when you went into the afterlife. Sometimes they even stashed away the fetuses of stillborn babies. Which brings us to this room. This is a preparation chamber. I've never heard of hiding one underground in a tomb, but it has to be. They got all the messy work done here. Mummification took months of work. Over there's the table where they embalmed you."

Charlie gestured with her flashlight over at a long stone pedestal near the far side of the room, standing almost waist height. More of the grates lined the base of it, sunken into a shallow channel. In the center of the table a knife glittered as it split the flashlight's beam into refracted lines on the far wall.

Norman made his way over while Charlie chattered merrily on. He had no particular desire to join in the conversation. Embalming had lost its charm when the doctors sucked the marrow out of Clara's bones, flooded it with lethal doses of radiation, and then pumped it back inside her. Not that it had done much good.

The room certainly did resemble a preparation chamber, but none of it really made sense. Tombs were always cramped and packed. Even if they allowed for a tiny annex chamber to finalize mummification, it should have been filled with jars of oils and incense. Open space was simply too expensive.

"They gutted and drained you. You have to get the fluid out for it to work. They even melted your brains and drained them out your nostrils, threw all the good stuff in a vat for drying and jarring. You got to keep your heart though, once it was jerky. They salted you, stuffed your corpse and packed you away. But that's not the half of it. Spending an eternity alone was unthinkable, so they'd sometimes mummify your servants and pets, living or dead, and send them along with you. And the men who built the tombs were often killed so they couldn't tell all the details of it. Occasionally they even killed the people who killed the builders."

The knife was a beautiful thing, a handle of bone notched and fixed with a blade of desert glass gone yellow with age and gently curved under its own weight.

Or it was almost beautiful, at least.

The blade was smeared red. The stone beneath it was wet.

Sieber made some sound—laughter or disgust—as Charlie gestured a frenzied pantomime, the shadows strobing strange flurries across the wall. She continued her rambling descriptions but Norman barely noticed. He felt as if he were underwater, moving impossibly slowly as he followed the trail of blood.

The smeared path continued across the table, down over the far edge, and spilled into a low stone vat that the workbench had hidden from sight.

And onto the boy.

CHAPTER

FOURTEEN

Charlie let out a wordless moan beside him.
The kid was a catastrophe of torn brown flesh, his naked body curled into a fetal position, knees squeezed tight against his scrawny, mutilated chest and open belly. Jagged lines crisscrossed unfamiliar symbols as they slipped through his skin, dipped down to slit open arteries and paint the basin red. His jaw stretched around a wad of drenched burial wrappings. His eyes stared an accusation toward heavens that could never answer one so far below.

He looked like a wrung-out rag.

Beneath him, at the bottom of the vat and gummed with gore, another grated tunnel sucked merrily at the last sticky trickle.

The four stood side by side, looking down at the mess.

"Who could have done this?" Norman finally asked.

"He did," Sieber said.

"He did this to himself?"

"Looks like it. See? He didn't cut his back or anywhere out of reach. Probably used the gag to bite down and fight through the pain so he could keep going before he passed out."

"Why?" Anita asked.

But Norman didn't know. If either of the others had an answer their faces sure didn't show it.

"Mr. Haas? A word?" Sieber's face was pale but his voice was steady. Norman wasn't sure whether to respect the man for his calm or to hate him.

He beckoned with his head and Norman followed a few steps away. Sieber set one meaty hand on Norman's shoulder and leaned in close enough that Norman could smell the stale coffee on his breath.

"We have a problem here."

"You think? Maybe… something happened, I don't know, he…"

But Norman didn't have to say it. Charlie already had. *They gutted and drained you. You have to get the fluids out to make it work…*

"You aren't hearing me. This wasn't some trap that got him, Mr. Haas. He bled himself. Or he was bled. And how long since we last heard him screaming? Twenty minutes ago? At most?"

"We must have just missed him. Maybe he heard us calling out and thought… I don't know, that we were some kind of curse?"

It sounded silly out loud but if it had been enough to scare Hazred away from a promise of riches, it might've been possible.

Sieber shook his head.

"The boy's been dead a while. Hours. Quite a few of them, I'd guess. He's stiff. The blood is gelled. It takes time. I know corpses and that isn't a fresh one."

Norman tried to process the man's words but found himself staggered instead with the thought that before that morning he had only ever seen one person die. His parents had passed without him there. One a stroke, the other a nursing home heart attack, both long gone before he arrived. He'd never stumbled on the body of a suicidal friend or witnessed some heinous accident. The bodies he had seen were all preserved and doll-like, reposed inside cushioned coffins or ancient stone boxes.

The only exception was Clara.

And now two fresh and grotesquely disfigured corpses.

"I don't understand," Norman said.

"I don't either."

"There's someone else down here, then?" Anita asked.

"I..." the big man faltered.

Anita grimaced.

"Look, I hate to interrupt the boy's club, but we're in this together. We all need to stay informed. If you have something to say, don't just tell Norman."

Norman glanced over at Charlie. The camera hung, frozen in her hands. She gazed into the vat, unblinking. She had not moved.

"This feels... organized," Sieber said. "We get lured down here by riches, by a child crying, by whatever it takes to get us in. Your boy Hazred closing the door on us, all of this. Something is very wrong here."

"He wasn't my boy," Norman said. "You think he's behind this?"

"It sounds a lot better than anything else I can think of."

"Did you hear that?" Charlie whispered.

"Hear what?" Sieber asked.

Norman didn't have to ask.

It could almost have been the sound of a faint and ragged wind, but it was not.

Kiya-Aten

The sound echoed up through the grate, followed by a distant thumping sound that echoed once, twice, again. It sounded like a drum. It sounded like a heartbeat. Dread climbed up inside

Norman's stomach, burning like the fingers of bourbon he'd downed the night before. Impossible.

The whispering faded into a memory. The drumming quieted until it could as easily have been his own blood pounding in his ears.

Anita stood beside him, slack-jawed, eyes wide in a disbelief that he knew and shared.

"Fuck this," Charlie said. "If there's anyone else down here, we'll come back for them. Bring the Army. Tear this place apart. We need to get out of here."

She licked her lips, turned and headed off for the nearest doorway at a pace just shy of a sprint. She climbed the staircase and vanished.

Sieber panned his flashlight back and forth across the other doorways. Each one led to level hallways, twisting off and out of sight. He frowned, shook his head.

"Ms. Levine? Charlie. Charlie, that's not the right way."

Only echoes answered.

Anita took off after her.

"Wait!" Sieber commanded, the sound offensively loud in the silence of the tomb. Neither woman returned. He turned to Norman. "We should stay here, wait until they come back. If we go running around…"

Norman knew he was right. Looking into the yawning mouth of the doorway, he knew he wanted him to be right, too. It was better to stay still. It was better to wait. It was the wiser choice. And if it were Clara down there in the dark, he never would have hesitated.

He followed.

His knees popped as he propelled himself up the steep stairwell, panting to pull in breath against the cold. He barked his shin on a jagged step. His head scraped the low-sloped ceiling and sent him stumbling to catch his balance. He fought back a panicked sound and reminded himself that he was safe, that it was all some bizarre misunderstanding, patiently waiting for him to figure out the answer. It sounded like a prayer, and he'd long since had his fill of praying.

A few dozen paces later, it split and dipped back downward.

Just as suddenly, Norman found himself alone on a cramped stone landing, hunching below a too-low ceiling to look down hallways that branched to his left and right. His pant leg was torn where he had hit the step. He could feel the bruising and the blood already, even if he could not see it.

The lightbox in the preparation room had not given much illumination, but alone in the ancient passageway, his red-stained flashlight helped even less. The world sunk into a shifting penumbra of stone and the obscenity of hieroglyphics that marred the walls. The sound of the others' voices echoed into a garbled, directionless mess that yielded no hint of orientation.

"Hello?" He called out.

Other voices echoed back.

Hello?

Norman?

Kiya-Aten…

And the sound of footsteps.

A toxic panic threatened Norman. Footsteps coming toward him. Alone in the dark. Senseless images rushing in waves, of gutted boys stumbling closer and closer through midnight paths. Of crushed men grinning through torn facades as they dragged themselves after him, hands slapping wetly on the ground.

"There you are," Sieber said. "Christ you move fast. I was just a step behind you starting out. And you didn't catch up with them?" He was breathing heavily as he crowded in close. Norman choked on his helpless terror before he finally managed to swallow it.

"I can't find them. I don't know which way…"

"Kill the light."

Norman did. The world immediately winked out into a darkness as thick as the stone above and below, a blackness so unrelenting it felt like a living weight pressing against him. If he had felt panicked and disoriented before, now he felt a simple awful weightlessness, as if he were falling into space, into an endless void that was neither empty nor benign. The voices continued their muddled dance. A distant reddish flicker reached him from the nearest hallway.

"That's our way," Sieber murmured. He flipped his flashlight back on and Norman did too.

They continued onward just long enough for Norman to wonder if they had made a dangerous mistake when the voices began to solidify.

"Charlie, listen!"

They burst around the corner to see the two women halfway down a straight corridor. The far end sloped downward and dropped away, and where the wall met the ground, more strange, ugly grates opened like mouths. Anita had her hand clamped around Charlie's wrist, was dragging her back toward Norman and Sieber. Charlie's nail polish glittered as she struggled.

"Get off of me! It has to be the right way. We came down stairs to enter the prep room, remember? There was only one staircase leading up."

And, oddly, Norman found himself agreeing with her. Everything felt unfamiliar and wrong, but only one of the doorways out of the preparation room had led upwards. He had a moment to consider it and then Charlie twisted her wrist and tugged free from Anita. Her momentum sent her backpedaling.

Charlie's foot came down.

CLICK

FIFTEEN

Charlie froze.

The CLICK rebounded, sharp and clear, pierced its way into Norman with a nearly physical force. He had a sudden vision of Calvin's corpse but with Charlie's pretty face instead, all crushed into gory putty.

"Go! Charlie, run!" Norman shouted.

Miraculously, she understood.

She dipped low to catch her balance and took off at a sprint toward the far end of the hallway, her feet pounding, flashlight panning and bouncing wildly as she fled.

She had nearly reached the end of the corridor when she snapped back as if punched in the face. She reeled, stumbled, and dropped to all fours. A strange, animal grunt, low and guttural escaped her. Only then could Norman see the wire above her, pulled taught at neck height, casting a blackline shadow against the ceiling.

It was dripping.

Charlie clawed at the walls to drag herself to her feet and looked back. The mask of shadows and feeble light could not conceal the confused terror playing across her face. One slim hand found her throat, but the blood continued to spurt through her fingers with wet heartbeat slops, drenching her vest in a soaked Usekh collar. She took a shambling step toward them. Her other hand extended, groped at the stained beam of light as if it were a rope that could pull her to safety.

Sieber took off running toward her. He made it nearly two steps when the slab above the trigger plate guillotined down from the ceiling. A third and he would have been pulverized, flesh and muscle mashed into a jelly of marrow and splintered bone. It slammed into place with an echoing thud that reverberated through Norman's gut.

Sieber hit the slab at a sprint, too late to slow his momentum, and bounced off. His arms pinwheeled in comical desperation and he flopped onto his back. Blood poured out of his nose unchecked as he scrabbled to his knees and clawed along the bottom of the stone wall that now bisected the passage.

"Charlie!" Anita screamed. Or maybe it was Sieber. Norman couldn't tell, couldn't make any sound at all either. The idea of breathing felt as foreign as the text on the walls, and, suddenly all he could think of was a fragment of a Psalm left over from so long ago: How shall we sing the Lord's song in a strange land?

"Keep pressure on your throat!" Sieber bellowed, his voice muddy and wet.

His fingers lodged in through the cracks in the grates and he strained, veins cutting their way along his forearms. Norman dropped to his knees beside the younger man and tried too, pulled upwards until his body shook and his vision burst into a nebulous of stars, but the stone didn't so much as shift. He collapsed back, his breath pluming clouds into the cold air with each shallow gasp. His head pounded and fingers stung. His heart beat dizzyingly hard. He tried again, Anita struggling beside him. The stone did not yield.

"Charlie, keep holding on," Anita said. "We'll be through in just a moment."

There was no response from behind the wall.

The urgent, desperate moments passed, stretched into minutes.

Norman sunk back on his heels, body shuddering from the strain. Anita got the crowbar and tried to use it for leverage, but the groove prevented any purchase. It rattled when it fell to the ground. Tears painted wet streaks down her cheeks that reflected the dim illumination of the flashlight. Sieber continued to struggle, but Norman found himself unable to do anything but sit and stare at the wall of stone.

Sieber swung the crowbar like a hammer, steel on stone ringing and spitting sparks like splinters of sun. They yielded little light. There was nothing to see, nothing beside the brief proclamation cut into the slab's face.

The same hieroglyphics written here, as before, the message hewn in stone without change or exception:

The rewards of Kiya-Aten, it promised, *are eternal.*

CHAPTER
SIXTEEN

The alarm for his gout medication rumbled beside him, pushing Norman awake.

He couldn't fully remember the dream he'd been having, but it was a troubling thing, an October seed born of panic and blood. A figure, tangled in linen, staggering under a silver moon across wind swept dunes like desiccated waves. A scent lingered too, something old and sour and rotten, smoldering incense and the moldering blankets under which he'd huddled after nightmares as a kid. He reached instinctively for his flashlight and flipped it on. Not that seeing yielded much comfort.

The monsters can't get you if the lights are on.

The thought came and left just as quickly. He'd seen the bright fluorescent lights on Clara's face. It hadn't stopped the flesh from melting away, day after day. The sunken eyes and cheeks, the bones stretching against cracked, flaking skin. All that light and her words had still dissolved into angry mumbling, confused, senseless as often as not as the chemo ate her brain.

His knees popped as he pushed himself to his feet. The years did not rest lightly. His legs and arms felt bruised, his hands were scuffed and sore and something in his back had shifted during the struggle with the stone slab. He rooted through his pockets until he found the day planner's stash of pills. He threw down the contents, dry, without checking which day.

The others didn't stir.

Anita was slouched against the wall, her head in her hands. Sieber dozed with the crowbar beside him, his beard matted with blood from his beaten nose. Neither seemed really asleep, but caught in the same dazed inebriation that had consumed Norman. They'd tried for hours. They'd struggled and raged and flailed against the unmovable object and Charlie... Charlie was still just gone.

He stumbled over to the slab.

Jerome had said she was supposed to be the future. Norman wondered what it was like for her to die there, alone, scared and hopeless, thousands of miles from home and family. If she had a family. He'd never really asked. He wondered what her parents would feel, if they were still alive, to know they had outlived their child. He didn't have to wonder very hard. He hoped they were dead.

Norman reached out and set one wounded hand upon the stone, expecting to find comfort in the coldness, but the slab was warm, the air redolent with the sharp, angry smell of blood. From Sieber's broken nose, Norman thought. He tried not to think about it too hard. The grate below his feet stretched to the far side of the slab and through it he heard the sound of a ragged catch of breath on the far side.

"Charlie?" he whispered.

But that couldn't be. Charlie was dead, had been dead for some time now. Even if they had somehow gotten to her she would not have survived.

Yet the feeling of a presence was unmistakable, a quiet looming thing so near that he could almost touch it. Something standing just inches away, on the far side of the wall, face pressed close to the stone as it sucked in breath and spat it back out.

Norman closed his eyes and concentrated. Underneath the stillness, he could hear the quiet rustle of cloth.

Like someone slipping through a lightless bedroom, maybe, trying not to wake her partner. Or bound in an anonymous cocoon of filthy burial cloth, skull grinning as she peered up through the walls of soil.

Norman trembled.

"Clara?" he asked, although he wasn't sure why.

The only answer was an oddly familiar sound that he could not quite associate with anything. The feeling of being watched receded and once again he was alone with his two companions, buried in stone beneath the sand and sky.

"Norman," Anita said. "Listen."

She pointed a trembling finger at the grate.

"Listen to what?" he asked. His heart was pounding in his chest, his bones felt heavy and soft inside his body, like gold. Like lead.

"Listen," she said again.

And then Norman heard it.

The whispering, endless sussuration of senseless words and sounds and beneath it all the heartbeat drumming repetition of a name. Her name.

Kiya-Aten.

"What does it say?" Norman asked.

Anita shook her head in slow, awful wonder. Norman wasn't sure if it was a denial or a refusal.

"What does what say?" Sieber asked. He looked up at the two of them, his brow furrowed in concern.

"You can't hear it?" Norman asked, but there was no need. If he heard it, he wouldn't have to wonder.

"Whatever you hear, it's probably just wind. There must be a hole to the surface somewhere or some trick they designed. We need to get out of here," Sieber said. He gripped the wall for support and dragged himself back upright. His rucksack scraped along the ground as he pulled it to him and threw it over his shoulder. "And we need to get working on that. Now."

It was only when Sieber moved the bag that Norman could place the sound he had heard before, as the presence faded away.

It was the sound of something being dragged.

SEVENTEEN

"Which way?" Sieber asked.

The small group had returned to the preparation chamber, and stood before the passageways. None of them looked remotely like the one that had first brought them down. Norman wondered why either of the other two waited on his answer. It wasn't like the rules of the expedition still applied, if they ever had.

"It doesn't matter," Anita said. "Didn't you hear her? Can't you hear her now? We're not going to get out of—"

"Let's try the left one. Keep going left. Eventually it should work out."

Sieber nodded. He led the way without hesitation.

The roads less taken, echoing with the distant whispers, swallowed them whole.

Norman's meager confidence in the plan dissolved almost immediately. The passages tangled in an intestinal, nonsensical sort of disorientation that immediately left him dizzy and short of breath. Staircases spilled upwards only to drop moments later, curving haphazardly and splitting like blood vessels in some strange dead monstrosity. Senseless picture sentences rambled across the walls in primal languages that seemed barely human.

After the first hour, claustrophobia began to set in. The darkness hung heavily and Norman's eyes ached from the constant red light, from fighting through it to scan the ground for loose stones that might signify a trap. The thought of the countless tons of sand and stone piled above him, around him, was no longer a bit of casual anxiety, it was a living oppressive thing that haunted and flung itself across the expanse of his mind. Down one corridor the walls squeezed into a point, until they had to shuffle, backwards, the way they'd come. The stink of sweat and fear from the others pressed more aggressively than the walls that brushed their foul and deranged writing up against his shoulders.

Norman shrank away from the hieroglyphics on them as if the fingers that had carved them lingered still, waiting to graze against him as he passed.

Down another corridor, on either side the floor slanted into tunneled pits so sharply that Norman was sure if he stumbled, he would slide down into the nameless bottomless black. His heart coughed and stammered as he hugged tight against the others and tried to look forward.

And then turning a corner, Norman found himself in an intersection once more, standing before the all too familiar mural with those caveman scrawlings whose eyes seemed to relentlessly pursue him.

"Did we get turned around?"

Sieber frowned at the wall.

"No," he said. He glanced at the compass, gave the glass a series of frustrated taps, and crammed it back into his utility vest. "Must be something magnetized nearby that is screwing with me. There's no way this is the same intersection. Let's keep moving."

They did.

More passageways, each branching off again and again, nothing to distinguish them from the next or indicate any progress besides an occasional grate, where rushing air—*just wind*, Norman insisted—seemed to whisper Her name. Sometimes Norman thought it sounded more like Clara and that only cut more sharply.

He could see it in the others. Sieber's shoulders hunched, vulture-like. He muttered frustrations and short angry sighs. Anita stumbled. She whimpered. She began to hum.

The third time they arrived at a muraled intersection, Norman stopped. A moment later, the others did too.

"This isn't working. We've been here before."

He knew the drawings, the eyes. Anita drifted, veering from wall to wall, peering at them without much interest. The song she was humming was familiar, for all she couldn't carry the tune. Steve Martin's "King Tut." Norman tried to find the humor in it.

"Don't think so. They're supposed to look the same. We came from a different direction than should be possible if it was the same as the last one. There's no way it looped around."

"Maybe there are two or three? We've been walking for hours. Even going slowly there is no way any maze of tunnels should be long enough to allow for that. It's just logistics."

Sieber tossed his rucksack on the ground and knelt beside it. He had a driven, obdurate look to him, his eyes narrowed with a tunnel focus.

"We don't have time for this. I'm telling you, it's not the same mural. Here," he said. He tugged out a pack of grease pencils and tapped one into his hand. He tore the string down through the layers of flaked wood. "If it makes you feel better, I can prove it.

The grease pencil left an ugly black scar across the hacked-in depravity.

Norman didn't object to the defacing.

They headed back into the breach, into the seemingly endless tangle, staircases climbing and falling, branching paths that led back onto themselves. New murals presented themselves at random intervals, each time branching into several paths. At each intersection, Sieber cut a waxy swath across the stone with the pencil, arrows and Xs, hieroglyphics of their own.

An hour passed. Then another. Then another. It felt like days. It felt like centuries. In the perpetual darkness and the tangled passageways of stone, time bled into itself, became trapped and lost as easily as the rest of them. Mural after mural, which Sieber smeared across as they passed, fathomless lengths of mobius strip corridor, tangled endlessly into a winding knot. They took breaks, the three of them huddled together and sipping from lightening canteens, but that was it. There was no food to spare, by Sieber's rationing.

"This is impossible," Norman gasped, at last.

Even Sieber looked winded.

Miles. Even if they were walking slowly, it had been miles at the very minimum. No tomb could be that big.

Norman dropped into a squat, hoping to yield some relief for his weary legs but mostly just causing his knees to let out pops that reminded him of a car's backfiring. He cradled his head in his hand for a long moment, sucking the bitterly cold air into his lungs.

If not, he might not have seen the tiny curls of wood scattered carelessly across the floor, paper thin and cocoon-like. They reminded him of toenails, or claws. Neither option made sense. Even if some stray animals had taken refuge in the tomb, he couldn't imagine any natural reason for wood to be down below the sand, miles of winding tunnel from the surface.

Norman picked one of the shavings up and crumpled it between his fingers. It was not some ancient fragment either, brittle with age. Confusion gave way to an awful dread that roped and coiled in his gut. He knew exactly what it was. The paper husk from Sieber's grease pencil.

"We've been here before."

"It's similar, but we've been marking each one off. It's gotta just be a massive network of tunnels."

Norman pointed at the small piling of shavings on the floor.

"No. It's not just similar. It's the *same*. We've been here before."

Sieber didn't argue it this time. He crouched down, ran his fingertips over the flaked wood. He looked up at the mural of atrocities engraved into the wall. The screaming half men. The lurid, perverted depictions of a population being torn apart one by one. And nothing else.

"Where's the mark?" he asked.

"It... I honestly don't know."

But that wasn't entirely true. He didn't know the specifics, but walls certainly didn't shed off grease marker on their own. Something was truly and terribly wrong. Whoever had called out earlier must be down there with them still, sneaking behind them and scraping off the evidence. Never mind that it was an unknown tomb in a forgotten corner of the world.

Or else it wasn't really a tomb at all, and that left only worse alternatives.

Anita let out a dry, retching cough that left her shaking and leaning against him for support. He struggled to not pull away even after he realized that it wasn't some contagious fit wracking her. It was almost like weeping, but Norman knew better. It was laughter.

CHAPTER
EIGHTEEN

Back in the preparation room. Again.

Half a day's worth of walking, of fumbling through the dark, and nothing to show for it except socks soaked a watery pink from macerations that his boots had etched into his ankles and the horrible reality that it might not actually work out okay. That there was a very real danger if they couldn't solve the problem soon. And that whoever was down there with them was pleased. Worse than nothing to show for it. Hopelessness hung about the others like a dimmed halo. Norman felt hungrier than he had in a long time.

They had walked outward for miles, but getting back to the preparation chamber was mercifully quick, only a few minutes. Norman thought it did not really feel much like mercy. It felt like inexorability. The insanity of it was muted by his weariness, but his mind still felt splintered at the edges. His pill timer gave its readout in radioactive, glowing letters, but it took Norman a long moment before he could make sense of the symbols. Numbers. Coming up on dawn. They had been searching for close to ten hours. It would be time to take his medication again soon. Hazred would begin preparing to leave. Charlie would be cold on the filthy floor. Stiff and blood turning to gel, like Sieber had said about the kid. He studiously looked anywhere other than toward the vat with the corpse inside it. Mostly, Norman wanted to eat. The wanting twisted in his stomach like something with claws. With teeth.

Norman watched with a sharp, manic sort of enthusiasm as Sieber laid out what food they had left: a bag of banana chips, a half pack of trail mix, and the three slabs of jerky that Norman had left in his pocket from the night before. The last two he returned to his rucksack. Norman swallowed down a throb of violent anger as it disappeared from sight. Strange, he supposed, that he should even care to eat given the circumstances.

He took the handful offering of banana chips with hands that trembled. He tried to savor it, to resist the urge to wolf it down, but in moments it was gone, his mouth chalky and teeth caked in the packed pastel-tasting sweetness. His stomach surged, hot and surly and he wondered for a moment, at what point he would need to take a shit. He had wanted so badly to be in textbooks for his discovery. He wondered if soiling himself in the preparation chamber would make a footnote if anyone ever discovered them.

"There's something odd going on," Sieber said, when he was finished.

Norman nodded. His hunger, momentarily lessened, let the rest of his discomfort shine even brighter. He slipped his boots off and massaged his ankles against the cold. Skin hung loosely, split and in flaps and stinging so sharply Norman had to fight back tears. The burst blisters made him think, for a moment, of that glance he had risked at Cal, after the bomb had gone off.

He took a deep breath and let it roll out, until the feeling passed. The boots were new, too. He'd bought them just for the trip. Had hoped—really hoped—that the cashier would ask him why he was buying them so he could tell her. It seemed an eternity ago. Anita held her chips like a handful of coins, rearranging them with a finger and flipping them one by one instead of eating. She looked hollow. Empty.

"She has so much to say," she mumbled. She cocked her head toward the grate.

The whispering was as bad as the tangled, impossible miles of maze. Sometimes it didn't sound like words at all, just rushing wind, like the whistle of bone chimes. Sometimes. Sieber was right. It had to be a trick. Another method to panic and disorient the intruders. When he held the thought, the whispering grew blurred and formless and he could almost pretend he hadn't heard it at all.

"Maybe it's meant to be like that. Functioning traps are a rare thing, but tombs often had labyrinths in them to keep out grave robbers. Everyone thinks of Crete when they hear labyrinth, but it started in Egypt. In the tombs."

"It's not a tomb," Anita corrected. Her voice carried none of her usual fire. "Not hers, anyway. It's written all over the walls."

"I don't think they designed it to keep us out," Sieber said.

"Hm?"

"Well think about it. The trap wall that came down. I don't think it was supposed to crush whoever triggered it. Your friend up there, Cal, he could've easily been standing around. The one that fell for Charlie, it was designed to fall behind whoever triggered it. That's not a deterrent, that's a way to keep people from escaping. Guessing a slab came down somewhere back there and is why we can't find the way out. It seems like we're walking in loops because the way out looks like a wall. It's an optical illusion of some kind, and it's screwing us over. If I knew where, I could try to chip away at it but if the grease pencil won't work, I've got no way of seeing which walls I've checked and which ones I haven't."

Norman decided to not press the implications of the erased grease pencil.

"Any more explosives?"

"No," Anita said. "Please no."

Sieber shook his head.

"I brought four sticks of PBX, and I used them all. I didn't think I'd have to blow up a metal bunker the size of Kentucky. Wouldn't do much good, anyway. If I can't tell where we are, I couldn't know how far away we are from the bomb. Wouldn't know where to put it either. Can't just wire up all of the walls."

Norman had a sudden image of the tomb rigged up to blow sky high and obliterate every trace of Kiya. Of Clara. Of himself. Anita had said it wasn't a tomb, but it was going to become one, at this rate. He wondered if the crater would be deep enough to see into the pits of biblical hell. See Hades sitting on his ebony throne. The thought gave him pause, and an idea.

"You can, though," Norman said. "That's how we can find our way out."

And it was true. The answer was right there. For the first time since he watched Charlie, still all blonde and pretty and full of potential, shuffle toward them as she drowned in her own blood, he felt hope.

Sieber waited for him to elaborate. Anita stared at the grate, the sand-colored chips still clutched in one hand.

"You're right. This is a labyrinth. The Labyrinth was a mythical maze where the Minotaur was kept, and it was designed to keep anyone who entered inside. Like you said. It wasn't really to keep them out, it was to make them afraid that if they entered you could never escape. You said you come prepared. You have cord or rope or something? A lot of it?"

"Of course. If you go anywhere without parachute cord, you're crazy."

"Tie it to that grate. Unwind it as we go. When Theseus entered the Labyrinth to kill the Minotaur, he used Ariadne's thread at the entrance to lead him back, but it's all the same as breadcrumbs."

Sieber frowned.

"It won't show us the way to the surface."

"It doesn't have to. It just has to show us everywhere we've been. It can't get confused or overlooked or erased, and if someone tries to change it, we'll know."

The man rummaged around in his pack. Norman turned to Anita.

He found it hard to speak, looking at her.

She rocked listlessly from one foot to the other. Her chin was dotted with crumbs.

"You'll be okay?" he offered.

She gave him an obedient attempt at a smile, but he could see tooth-cut trenches in her lips, the smear of red like lipstick from nervous chewing. Her eyes seemed empty. The subservience worried him the most.

"Four spools, two hundred meters a piece. That's half a mile's worth. Should at least take us part of the way."

Four packets of olive-dyed rope, bound around themselves like packed away Christmas lights. That was their best chance at escape. He tried not to think too hard about the futility of the situation, about the miles of desert sand, of stone, of far distant help that hadn't even yet begun to search for them. About the ruin of Anita, nodding blankly along to… whatever, simply because at some mortal extreme, any sort of obedience was easier than struggle.

"Let's go, then."

The cold air stung at Norman's ankles, but sliding the boots back on was far worse. The rigid folds settled back into their trenches and immediately began to saw away. Norman shook as he found his footing, but after the first step it got easier. Things always did.

The first spool led them to a staircase. The second spool led them back to the muraled intersection.

They stopped there for a moment as Sieber made a miniature noose to grip the knotted end of the next spool.

"Which way? We're at half our distance."

A quarter mile from the preparation room, from the stinking body of the boy. From the grate where the end of the olive cord looped and dangled down into the unforgiving grip of shadow. He tried to calculate where another quarter of a mile would place them, but it was a meaningless effort. It could as easily leave them on the surface as at a second intersection, for all he could tell.

Norman studied the wall. He couldn't see anything useful in the hideous grotesquery, but between the murky light and the mind-staining weariness it would have been hard to read direct instructions in English. He waved Anita closer. She took a step closer and lingered at the far end of the intersection.

"Can you read this all enough to see if it gives any clues?

Anita shivered. She gave them a reluctant glance and then went back to staring at her feet.

"Bits and pieces. Most of this writing is told by context and this is all… nonlinear. I don't feel so good. Can't you all hear that?"

Norman looked back the way they'd come.

He could hear it, still. Not clearly, but the distant thrilling pulse of drums, the faint whisper slipping through the depthless darkness, as ragged as split fingernails.

"I think I can," he said. "We'll get through this. We're getting out of here, Anita. Just… try."

He wasn't sure what he was asking her to try. She gave him a miserable look, eyes sunken and face waxy. Sieber clapped her on the shoulder in some attempt at comradery.

"It's just the wind. Like I said, that's good news. It may mean we have a way out. Keep it together."

She sank away from him.

"How... moving..." she whispered.

Sieber sighed, let his hand drop to his side.

"I'm just trying to help, lady."

But Norman saw it too. The parachute cord was moving.

It slithered gently, steadily, away from them, the slack along the ground diminishing little by little. The spool began to turn. Sieber unhooked it from his belt and held it up to the flashlight. He stopped it.

"Huh," he said.

The cord gave a final slight tug before going limp. Norman wondered what Theseus had thought, plunging through the labyrinth with the Minotaur ahead, the abomination gorged on hatred and blood as it shuffled through the dark toward the intruder.

Then the rope snapped taut and the spool flipped out of Sieber's hands, rolling as it unreeled, bouncing and skittering across the stone and down the hallway behind them.

NINETEEN

"Stay behind me," the big man said.

Gun in hand, he stood between them and the darkness beyond. The flashlight on his utility vest pressed feebly into the endless black, split against the weapon and cast twin shadows that reached along the walls like outstretched arms. The darkness pressed back.

"Don't chase it," Norman said.

He wasn't sure what else to suggest. Sieber ignored him. Anita had her eyes squeezed shut. She mouthed silent prayers in strange languages.

"If you're there, now's the time to come on out," Sieber said. His finger slipped into the trigger well.

The spool rattled in the distance, clacked over stone, and then stopped. A hundred yards, Norman guessed. Maybe two hundred. The way the passageways twisted and split, it was impossible to tell.

The only answer was that strange thrumming, growing closer with each step, and the rasp of whispered words, unknown.

"Maybe it's a friend of the boy," Norman said, but he knew it wasn't. He huddled closer to the others.

The three of them advanced, pace by pace, clustered tightly enough that Norman could smell the stink of fear in their sweat. He was limping. He shivered against the cold.

At the first branch, Sieber took a right, up a small flight of stairs and into a stretch of hallway that looked almost familiar. There he stopped.

"Careful," he said. "See those grooves in the wall? The grate? This looks just like the place Charlie died. There may be a trigger switch. You two hang back a step or two."

"It doesn't just look like the place Charlie died. It *is* the place Charlie died," Norman said. It was easier to notice it now that he knew what to look for. The divot in the stone where Sieber had thrown down his crowbar. The splash of blood from his broken nose. Norman had hoped to leave no trace, when they arrived. He was suddenly glad for his failure. The air was warmer, here, his breath leaving only the faintest trace of fog. "Might have even been where Cal died. We've been acting like this place is huge, but maybe it isn't. Maybe it isn't that big at all."

"Where's the slab?"

Norman shook his head. The trap had been reset.

"This hallway shouldn't be here," Sieber said, when no one answered. "We didn't come this way."

Norman could hear the surrender in his voice.

"It's moving," Anita whispered again. "She's moving it. We're being herded."

"Sieber, I don't think we should go down that way," Norman said.

He tried to keep his voice calm. If the man insisted on going, he decided, he would do so on his own. Anita let out a gagging hack, bent over her knees and spat fruitlessly onto the ground. At the far end of the sloping corridor, the floor dipped sharply downward. The wire that had cut into Charlie's throat scored a sharp line above it. The floor was stained dark, but there was no trace of Charlie's body.

Sieber stared it down as if it were a feral animal, red in tooth and claw. He gave a slow nod.

"Okay, boss. Okay. We'll go back," Sieber said at last. He did not lower his gun or turn away as they backpedaled toward the stairwell.

CHAPTER
TWENTY

The sarcophagus squatted in the center of the preparation chamber, gleaming faintly in the light box's pale swath of radiance. It no longer seemed pretty.

Norman sat down with his back to it, let his head rest against the cold metal. The awful chill crept in through his scalp but it helped ease his pounding headache. Anita tossed her pack on the ground beside him and laid down, using it as a pillow. Her eyes were dark and troubled, sunken into her skull. She was sweating. Sieber leaned back against the wall across from them. He seemed reluctant to enter the room. Norman could understand why.

The boy's corpse was missing. The vat had been emptied while they hunted, no trace left behind but a stain. A frayed scrap of parachute cord remained knotted to the grate beside it, dangling into empty space.

"Maybe your Minotaur got him," Sieber suggested. He ran a hand over his scalp.

Norman wasn't sure if he was trying for humor.

"Maybe it did."

"So, tell me about her," he said at last. Now that he was no longer a prisoner of the cramped corridors, a fragment of his confidence had returned.

"Who?"

"This Kiya person who was buried here. I might as well know who built this nightmare. I've never heard of her."

"She was a princess," Anita whispered. She stared down into the grate, eyes open and glazed.

"That's a theory," Norman said.

Anita continued as if he hadn't spoken.

"She was taken from her homeland in Mitanni, sold in a peace treaty that would be forgotten years later. She travelled those awful months and miles across the open desert to be the bride of a pharaoh she'd never met. Yet she loved him. She served him. She carried his daughter. And she was betrayed."

Sieber shot Norman a curious look. Norman shook his head. The woman shuddered and her eyes slipped closed. Her breath came shallow, rasped like the whisper wind that hissed through the dull metal bars.

"Not much is known about her," Norman said. He kept his voice quiet. If Anita was asleep, he'd rather keep it that way. She needed the sleep, and something about her emotionless drawl made his heartbeat feel sharp and hollow. "A few images and references. Mostly her involvement with the Atenist heresies."

"The what?"

"The Pharaoh Akhenaten believed that the Egyptian gods besides Aten weren't supreme deities, but more akin to… demigods. He said they shouldn't be worshipped, that Aten alone was a true God.

"It was not a popular belief. Brought about the end of a dynasty. Arguably of all Egyptian dynasties, since they never really seemed to recover. After Akhenaten died, they tried to re-establish the old relationship with their religion but it didn't come back quite the same way. The gods no longer seemed to answer prayers and people lost interest. Kiya was Akhenaten's second wife. She whole-heartedly supported him and led the Atenist movement. By the time he died, she had disappeared. They etched her off the history books entirely, for her blasphemies."

"Akhenaten was important?"

"They conspired against her. They took her child. They raised up in rebellion. So, she ate the offering at the oracle of Amun," Anita whispered. "She ate the flesh of a god. 'And close your eyes with holy dread…'"

Her voice was so quiet and lips so still that Norman wasn't sure, at first, that she was speaking. He wanted to reach out and give her shoulder a squeeze, but he wondered, for one awful moment, if he would find her skin as cold as stone, her body a bag of sand and dust. He pushed the thought aside, concentrated as best he could on Sieber's question.

"Yes. Extremely rich, extremely powerful. You'd know him as the father of Tut. Kiya was Tut's stepmother," Norman said. "She may have been a foreigner, but it's not really known. As for what the blasphemies she committed were… well, that's not really known either. But Anita is right. Hazred's text from Amarna seems to say she ate an offering to Amun. Amun was one of the primary gods the movement scorned."

"…for she on honeydew hath fed…" Anita mumbled in response.

Norman tried very hard to ignore her. He knew what line came next in Coleridge's poem, but he had an immediate, irrational fear that hearing it out loud would make it all too hard to deny.

"And that's all?"

Norman nodded again.

"...and drunk the milk of paradise."

"Sure. Okay. She went and ate something from a church and they tried to un-person her? Why is she here, then?"

"Supposedly she fled after her crime. She took a load of her husband's money and a few loyal subjects. It wasn't just something that she ate though. Offerings were more than that. They set up altars and laid out wines, flowers, bread, honey. Meat. In their religion, those offerings became the body of the gods they were laid out for. You could lure them in with gifts and they would manifest. You could even trap them..." He trailed off.

You could trap them with gold... and silver. *A place once so plentiful in silver...* He didn't have to reread Clara's letter to check. He knew it by heart. He also knew where the silver from those ancient mines had gone and why Kiya had chosen this of all places.

Sarcophagi came in layers. The outer one was the sturdiest line of defense, then smaller more intricate ones as each fit inside the others like nesting dolls. And engraved with mazes to keep the soul from escaping before judgment. The golden coffin behind him wasn't the outer layer of anything at all, unless he missed his guess. Sieber's explosive failed because of a metal wall. The entire tomb was a sarcophagus with a shell of silver, and they had slipped to the furthest depths.

"You mean she ate a god by eating a handful of flowers? Some bread? And you think that's how she's doing... whatever she's doing to us? That's the stupidest thing I've ever heard."

"You said you're a Christian. You ever had Communion?" Norman asked.

Sieber frowned.

"It's not the same."

"You sure? Seems like you were also sure about Hazred locking us down here, and I think it's safe to say that he wasn't the one that closed that door on us."

"Please stop," Anita said. "Please just stop talking. Please leave me alone."

Norman sighed. It was too exhausting to argue. God's failures weren't Sieber's anyway. At least the man tried.

"She's right. We should get some rest," Sieber said. His irritation seemed to have evaporated as quickly as Norman's had. "We've got limited supplies and quite a few problems to figure out, but running around and panicking won't help. We aren't making Hazred's deadline, if he's even still up there. That's just that. Maybe he didn't lock us down here after all. Maybe it was this Kiya person, but I'm guessing he didn't linger once the door closed. We should sleep while we can. I'll keep first watch."

"Watch against what?" Norman asked.

It was a pointless question and Sieber ignored it. Anita simply smiled and buried her face deeper into her backpack. She began to snore almost immediately.

The light box flickered, guttered. Sieber slipped a new battery pack from his rucksack and set it beside the box. "I'll wait until it's out to switch it. We don't have a third. You think she's okay?" he asked.

"Sure," Norman said. He paused and then shook his head. "No. Are any of us? What's the plan?"

Anita shivered, moaned in a language he did not recognize.

"Maybe it's time we stopped running and went looking for this Kiya. Get some sleep," Sieber said. He leaned back against the wall and let his eyes hang half shut.

Norman eased down against the bitterly cold stone, felt it dig into his hip, his elbows, his shoulders, reviving old aches and forgotten pains, fanning the dead embers to life.

His head still hurt from the bomb. His arms and legs throbbed from exertions. His ankle felt like it was being eaten by something acidic. He was old, his body beaten, but looking at Anita made him feel even worse. She was young. Not a child, like Charlie, but she was still so much younger than him. Sieber was here as his job, Norman was here because it was the only place he could go, but she shouldn't have come. He could have gone with a larger group, torn the house of Kiya-Aten apart, let her study the remains piece by piece. He had done this to her.

She moaned. It was an awful, pitiful sound. This time he forced himself to rest a hand on her shoulder and found it only flesh and bone. Chilly, but not inhuman. He almost felt ashamed of himself for wondering.

He gave her a firm shake to drag her out of her nightmare.

Her eyes snapped open immediately, lips peeled back and teeth bared. Her cheeks were hollowed into corpselike emaciation by shadows. For a moment, she was grotesque. For that moment, she was awfully familiar.

"It's okay," he whispered to her. "It's going to be fine."

"Norman?" she whispered. Her breath left a puff of mist like a ghost between them.

All the languages she knew failed her and she shuddered wordlessly, helplessly, underneath his hand.

"It'll be alright. Everything will be fine," he said.

She didn't need to shake her head or respond. They both knew he was lying.

"I'm sorry," he said. "You were right. I'm the reason we're here. My expedition. I didn't think... I didn't know."

Anita said nothing, but she did not pull away from him. She pressed up close and he held her, feeling the warmth of her body against the awful cold, the smell of her hair like cinnamon and sweat, the same as before the nightmare began, when they'd all been packed tight in the straining Jeep.

In the failing light, he could almost believe she was someone else.

CHAPTER
TWENTY-ONE

He woke up, alone, to the sound of sobbing. "Clara?" he mumbled, before he could catch himself. She'd cried a lot near the end. While she still had tears left. He blinked away the daze.

Something else too, besides the weeping. Dripping.

The dim LED lamp made only feeble efforts to fight off the suffocating darkness, and it took Norman several minutes to orient himself. A lump of shadow against the far wall rose and fell with even breaths. Sieber must have fallen asleep, Norman supposed. He looked around for Anita but she was nowhere in sight. The filthy stone ground beside him was cold. He forced himself to tired, battered feet. His back and hips ached in bruised protest.

It didn't take him long to find her.

She was hunched over the grate beside the cleaning vat, where the boy had lain, and her body hitched and rocked within the shadow it cast.

"Anita?" Norman whispered.

"She won't stop. She won't ever stop."

"Won't stop what?"

He fumbled for his flashlight, raised it and clicked it on.

Anita shrank away from the beam, wrapped her arms around herself and huddled closer to the vat. Her eyes caught the light and glinted from their sunken places, the eyes of a feral animal peering up at him, mortally wounded, from the side of the road.

Her clothing was a sodden mess around her feet. She was naked.

The grate beside her glistened darkly with pooled blood.

"These things she's saying. This is what she does..." Anita mumbled.

She extended one arm, torn and gouged from her palm on up with a familiar symbol, the same name that echoed up from the grate, hoarse and hungry and furious. Wet streaks made forked, lightning paths down her wrist, collected on her fingers before spilling off into space. She twisted her hand back over the grate and clenched it until she shook, feeding the trickle down into the metal mouth.

"...what she needs..."

The grate steamed from the heat, so like a breath.

"...look what she's become..."

Anita stood up. It wasn't just her arm carved into bleeding tattoos. They scrawled insane pathways down the gentle slope of her small breasts, down across her belly and cut trenches into the wiry thatch of pubic hair. They etched brutal angry claims down her thighs.

"Oh Anita," Norman said. He took a step toward her but couldn't think of any way to help. Even her cheeks were dimpled with cuts, her neck raked as if it had been clawed by some bizarre, primeval beast. He bent down to gather the sodden mess of her clothing. "Anita, listen to me. It's going to be okay. Here's what we're going to do. We're going to find Kiya. We're going to make this all stop. It's going to be—"

"Put it down."

Sieber's voice was quiet, but the mild tone was more jagged than if he'd bellowed the command. Norman had not heard him rise. Had not seen the sacrificial blade pressed flat against the crisscrossed meat of Anita's thigh, either.

Anita's sobbing stopped. She looked between the two of them, glassy-eyed and without recognition. She let out a humorless giggle.

"Do you hear what I hear?"

"Anita," Norman said. "Anita, you don't need the knife."

"Put it down," Sieber said again. The voice of an automaton.

"Always talking, always whispering. That awful river, it never stops. Even when I'm dreaming. Am I dreaming? He woke her, you know. Cal did. She built this place herself over centuries. She had slept for so long, but it only takes a couple drops to wake her, and she thirsts. How can she not? It's all she knows. She might've gone back to sleep, too. But the boy... the bomb... Charlie..."

Norman rose from his crouch, slowly. He stretched his hand out toward her. He tried not to think of the razor edge whisking through flesh and tendon, the spurt of blood, the blazing sting as he came apart.

Anita looked down at herself, at the sacrilege of her body. She let out a low and hollow sigh.

"Please don't, Norman. I don't want to hurt you. I never would. But we entered her house. No one leaves her house. Not until she's satisfied. She needs more..."

"Now," the big man ordered.

Anita stiffened.

Norman's fingers brushed her wrist and the spell unwound. She looked up and her eyes guttered with wild, rabid rage. Her shoulder slammed into his chest as she flung herself past him.

Norman fought to keep his footing but the ground was slick with her blood and he went down hard.

The corner of the golden sarcophagus hit his temple and then everything was muffled, strange and distant, a heap of broken images.

Anita bounding toward Sieber like a blurred shadow, the knife slicing glittering ribbons through the darkness.

The tiny woman's momentum propelling them into the chamber's wall.

A flashlight shattering.

Strange purpling darkness exploded across his vision, choked out even the pale LED box's glow.

Vertiginous pain came in waves and then receded, only to come again.

Norman's cheek pressed against the grate, the cold metal digging in and only then did he realize he was on the ground. He squinted through the bruised façade but could make little sense of the furious tangle of their bucking bodies. He probably needed to get up. To fight or help.

He made it half way to his knees before his body stopped responding to such mild-mannered requests.

They were fighting.

He could hear them.

The grunts and growls like animals in heat. The smack of meat. The shrilling pain in Sieber's voice. The sound was loud enough to make Norman tremble. Any louder, and he thought his skull might split open.

The two shadows parted. Anita hit the ground only a few feet away from Norman. She skidded, rolled and sprang back to her feet. Norman could see her smile. She wore gloves of glistening red. She took off running.

Norman's world exploded in a supernova blast of sound and furious light and then a ringing silence, the trilling of a hospital alarm flatlining in his ear.

Darkness came, and swiftly.

CHAPTER
TWENTY-TWO

*S*he stumbled down the hallway, a shambling, awful figure, flesh turned black with age and exsanguination, the shriveled pucker of her mouth peeled back over rotten teeth. The wet stench of her billowed in a foul parade, despite the wrappings stained in blood countless centuries old. Her hands groped in the dark as she shuffled, the cloth wrappings dangling, tattered, as she blindly advanced.

Norman watched as Sieber tried to run but there was something wrong with his stomach. He doubled over, clutching at his abdomen, and his fingers sank inside himself like stone into sand. She gripped him with careless, implacable strength. Long bony fingers wiggled free of the wrappings and worked their way into the soldier's eyes and mouth. He did not scream. He simply let out a wet sigh and collapsed.

She turned to Norman and that ruined mouth smiled, eyes gleaming faintly through gaps in the cloth.

A sentence of garbled sounds whispered out but beneath it all, the throbbing of his heart beat in time: Kiya-Aten. Kiya-Aten. Kiya-Aten.

She reached up and began to unwind the wrappings, and he could not look away. Beneath, it was not a stranger's face that the corpse wore, not some visage forgotten since the fall of the Pharaohs.

It was Clara's.

Norman startled awake, and immediately began to retch. He choked and sputtered on the sound, tried and failed to get it under control.

Anita.

For an awful terrifying moment, he imagined her hunched in the dark, just out of sight. Grinning with ancient hate, the glass-bladed butcher's knife in her hand, ready to tear out his entrails and prepare him for the tomb. He needed to be quiet.

Except, he realized, it wouldn't matter. He would have no chance of hiding or fighting. The younger woman would have been more than his match even if he weren't so weak and wounded.

Everything hurt. His hip and shoulder were bruised, heavy, flesh saturated with pooled blood. His breath came sharply against wounded ribs, but far worse was his head. He touched the side of his face and felt thick coagulation making a gummy ridgeline across his scalp. The warm trickle across his cheek could have been tears or blood. He felt cold to his core.

He dragged himself along on all fours out from behind the sarcophagus and toward the LED box. Sieber lay on the far side of it, against the wall. The gun was on the ground beside him. His eyes were closed.

Norman waited on his hands and knees, feeling pitifully helpless and hung over, until the sensation of spinning slowed down.

"Sieber?" He whispered. It felt wrong to profane the silence of the tomb.

Kiya-Aten, the faint echo answered.

"Mm," the big man said. His eyes slowly opened.

"You doing okay?"

Kiya-Aten, Kiya-Aten...

"Been better. Man, your girl fucked me up," he said. "Your head doing okay? Saw you took a pretty bad clip there. Heard you mumbling in your sleep so I figured you weren't dead."

Norman squinted over at the lump in the doorway, her brilliance smeared in a blackish starburst on the wall above her head. The knife lay beside her, caked with so much more than just blood.

"Anita wasn't my girl."

It was all he could think to say.

"I didn't mean Anita. Your girl." He waved a hand vaguely, an all-encompassing gesture. "She's doing this somehow."

"What do you mean?"

"You know what I mean. Kiya-Aten," he whispered.

Kiya-Aten answered the tomb.

"You can hear it too, then?"

"Of course I can. I just figured it was a trick, didn't want to play into the hysteria. And I can drown it out. Guess Ms. Sidhu couldn't."

"Anita could understand it. How do you drown it out?"

Sieber shrugged and then winced.

"SERE school, I guess. Focus hard enough on something else and anything becomes a blur. Works for resisting interrogations. Works with wives too."

Neither laughed at the joke. Norman lowered himself against the cold metal sarcophagus until he was sitting upright. His vision blurred in and out of focus of its own accord, vertical neon streaks dancing, dizzying and half seen, in the corner of his eye. The ache in his head throbbed with unforgiving power.

"You have a wife?"

"I've had a couple."

"Kids?"

"One."

"Boy? Girl?"

"Does it matter?"

Norman had no answer.

"What do we do now?"

Sieber sucked a breath in through gritted teeth and let it slowly escape in a ghostly fog.

"We? I don't know, brother. I think you go on down and find her. Cut this bitch down. Take my gun and drop as many rounds in her as you can. You know how to shoot?"

Norman shook his head and nearly vomited from the sensation. He focused on the coldness of the air and tried to ignore the slippery wet warmth that trickled from his ear down to his chin.

"What about you? What will you do?"

"Me? I think I'll stay here. Might even crawl inside that pretty gold box. It was designed for a god, you said. Good enough for me."

If the man was joking, he gave no sign.

Norman opened his mouth to protest, to tell him that he was going to be okay, but what was the point? Like Bob Dylan said: Let us not talk falsely, now—the hour's getting late. Sieber wiped at his mouth and took a swig from his canteen.

"Fuck rationing," he said. He sputtered and coughed, his hand pressed tight against his sodden shirt. The water that dribbled from the corner of his mouth stained his beard as dark as plum juice.

After the fit passed, he continued. His breathing was ragged.

"Angelica."

"Pardon?"

"My daughter. That's her name. You got any?"

"Never really found the time. This was always our child, Clara's and mine. Ancient Egypt." He intoned. He raised a hand and then dropped it. "I was raised on this. I've been reading about this place for fifty years."

"Shit's not like the books, is it?"

"No, I suppose shit is not," Norman agreed. "Your daughter should be proud of you. You're a good man."

Sieber let out a harsh laugh that strangled off as he pressed his hand against his stomach.

"You're a long way from home."

"If I can stop her, maybe we can get you out of here."

"And what, walk miles across a desert to try for the nearest doctor? If this happened back home or if I could call in a medevac, fine. But in this place... I'm done. You know it as well as I do. It's too cramped, I let her get too close. Should've just shot her when I saw the knife. Here." He shoved the gun across the floor. It made it almost half the distance. "She fucked us up good. Go on and fuck her up right back."

CHAPTER
TWENTY-THREE

They ate the last of the food together, a final meal of tasteless, salty tongues of meat jerky and peanut-heavy trail mix, and then Sieber went quiet and Norman began collecting his things. The other man's breath whistled wetly. He did not open his eyes. He did not speak again.

There wasn't much to collect.

He took the vest light from Sieber's vest and the rest of the water that would have been Anita's. He took the gun. His pill timer must have broken during the fight, the radio-active green now dark. He doubted he needed to worry about keeping up with his medication.

The vest light was nowhere near as bright as his flash-light had been, but there was nothing to see anyway and Norman knew where he was going. He made his slow, limping pace past Anita's body and up the staircase of roughly hacked stone. He doubted it really mattered which stairwell he took, sooner or later they would lead him where he needed to go.

It didn't seem to take long, although Norman had very little conception of time. It seemed as much prey to Kiya as anything else.

He stood at the corridor where Charlie had run, that mad-dash frenetic sprint toward her sudden end. It was difficult to see the trigger plate in the muted light, but Norman was very patient. The grates on either side exhaled a faint fog of warmth, their chants swelling at his approach.

He'd heard Clara moving down this way, after Charlie died. Kiya, he corrected himself. Not Clara. He found himself scratching the symbol of her name against his palm as he stepped over the trigger. He ignored the grates and the voices within them. Focus on something else, Sieber had said.

Norman was familiar with the distortion of time.

Clara's deconstruction had taken years that slipped by in a flicker, yet were bricked together from days that felt endless. Even his life felt as if a joke had been played on him at some point, some hoax where the magician gave his knowing wink to the audience after the volunteer vanished into thin air and the crowd gasped with delight, certain that the missing one was only gone for a little while, that he would return soon. It felt like he was a child just days ago. When had he become middle aged? How did they steal his youth?

The air grew warmer, as he walked, and the murmur of voices became a cacophonic echo as it billowed and blasted against him from every angle with awful, hateful force. If there were any doubt that Kiya was awake, it dispelled just as easily as sun-scalded fog.

Norman felt himself tremble. He tried not to think. He forced a step, then another. Past a smear that stained the stony floor. Past the streak where a body had been dragged. He came to the wire that had cut Charlie open and he ducked beneath it. It snagged at his hair with jagged barbs. His back moaned in protest.

Only a few steps more and he reached the staircase at the end of the hallway.

The throbbing chant reached a disorienting height, overwhelming. Norman grit his teeth against the dizziness, the sensation of diminishing with each step as the voice grew louder and louder. He knew he wasn't far away.

"You have to be ready," he whispered to himself. "Because it's time."

"It's too soon." His voice was a whisper, struggled even with that. "We got this. We can beat this."

Clara patted his hand with one withered claw. She was so small and sickly, scalp scabbed and skin loose. Her whole body had melted like a wax doll to some primordial essence beneath. A classroom skeleton that breathed and spoke. Horrifying and pitiful. Most days she barely recognized him, her brain fried by the poisons and by the endless struggle. Most days he barely recognized her.

Today she watched him with clear, lucid eyes sunken deep in their caverns. The room still stank of human waste and antiseptics.

"No," she murmured. Her lips were cracked and pale, blended into her face. Lips he'd once kissed, that had glibly mouthed such filthy things while he fumbled through his wedding vows. Lips he had felt pressed against his bare skin in sweaty darkness. The memory felt profane. "Norman, I tried."

They both had. For years.

It hadn't been all bad. There had been remissions. There had been ups and downs. There had been hope.

Each round of chemo broke against her like waves against a beach, eroding only a little at first, then more and more.

The last round of chemo was the hardest. She dissolved before his eyes. Every day more confused. Stared senselessly into space. She drooled. Had no bowel control. Said horrible things to the nurses. Screamed out in misery when she could. Worse still, was when she would lay, soundless, mouth agape and eyes wide open in a silent display of agony that would continue for hours no matter what he said. Sometimes he wondered if she would ever stop, or if they'd bury her that way, her body too broken for screaming and forever trying.

"I'm not ready. Honey, I can't do this without you."

He wasn't sure what that even meant. His whole life had been infected with her cancer.

The passions they'd shared for three decades—for Egypt, for the University, for her research into the lost queen Kiya—all seemed a distant memory of a past life. And for nothing. She was done. Giving up.

He could not meet her gaze. He stared instead at a plastic plant by her bedside, stiff and eternally green.

"You have to. You have to be ready because it's time. I'm tired. I can't win. I don't even want to, anymore. We did our best. I want you to keep on going."

And he had agreed. How could he not? It was an awful command, but it was one he couldn't refuse.

He kept on going.

CHAPTER
TWENTY-FOUR

A dull, madder glow painted the steps below him and all his certainties trembled. Sweat spilled from pores and cut paths through the filth and grime that had collected in a shroud over him ever since entering the tomb.

Not far at all.

It was why he'd come, he reminded himself. Sieber was right. And Sieber was dead and no amount of reasoning could help Norman put aside the feeling of terror and awe, a desire to throw himself on the ground and howl out in worship of something far less than divine until at last his end found him.

The gun was heavy, clammy, the handle slick where he gripped it. Instead of a feeling of security or power, the weight of it felt impotent. Like he was some primitive half-man, holding a stone and scraping onto the walls an image of fire and stars.

The light pulsed and throbbed as it climbed up his body with each descending step. The air grew warmer, more humid. It smelled of hot metals and smoldering incense.

The stairwell opened up into a corridor. Not a winding branching path like those ways above, but a straight wide hallway all the more terrible for its simplicity. At the end, a doorway. Beyond the door, a pedestal. The dull red glow spilled out from atop the pedestal like blood from a wound, soaking the clutter of peculiar, gleaming shapes that littered either side of the passageway and crowded toward the path.

Sarcophagi of gold and silver, sealed, lay end to end on either side. Between them, statues of the same precious metals, contorted and demented, body parts swapped and strewn about in a bizarre array of tangled limbs and random likenesses. Other lesser murdered things, too. Bony wreckage, leathery desiccated husks turned papery with age. He could feel their eyes watching him as he passed.

Norman peered down at the nearest mangled statue, a man with the head of a dog. The arms and legs had been torn off and stacked beside the torso, and the golden ribcage jutted, gnawed and bent, over an empty black pit where the viscera would have lain. It still looked wet.

The dog's face, even in death, was frozen in an unmistakable look of terror, the gemstone eyes riveted on Norman.

Not a dog, Norman realized. Not random either. A jackal.

The gun fell from his hands, struck the ground with a dull, echoing clatter. He didn't stoop to retrieve it. It had no power here, he knew.

Beside the dog-man's corpse, the body of a cow, carved from gleaming precious metals, spattered in gore that never dried. The gilded husk of a crocodile came next, torn in half. On each sarcophagus he found a name too. A likeness. Figures that Norman recognized as easily as childhood friends. Anubis. Osiris. Horus too, and Hathor and Thoth. Amun-Ra. Between each sarcophagus, the countless lesser gods whose names he could no longer recall grew more and more cluttered, piled in drifts as deep as snow. He wondered if Charlie was among them. Calvin, too, and the kid. Gutted, chewed and discarded. Bone and gristle, silver and gold. The mausoleum of a pantheon, frozen in their death as they watched Norman pass by and toward the doorway.

Toward the Eater of Gods.

Upon the walls, a sprawling tale of symbols that he could not read, only now he knew who wrote them. Not a scribe at all, just as there had been no trained builders, at least not below the temple's outer layer. He didn't need to read them. He knew what they would say.

How She lured the gods with their idols and treasures and invocations. How She stalked them through the shifting labyrinth that she had built and bent with her own hands, catching and tearing them open and devouring them as they wearied while trying to flee. Consuming their gifts and godhood until it simmered inside her. First the offerings from the oracle at Amun, fragments of divine favor, and then the lesser gods. Small and helpless ones. Then bigger, and bigger, any she could trap inside, the abomination of her heresy growing in scale with each act along with her capabilities, a culling of Aten's contenders, of anyone who strayed into her snare.

The door at the end yawned wider and from inside he heard the rustle of ancient fabrics, the rasp of breathing, as jagged as the teeth of a saw. Her heartbeat was a drum louder than his own. The chanting in his mind reached a feverish wail.

Kiya-Aten! Kiya-Aten!

And yet Norman found himself lost in a memory of tile floors and fluorescent lights, of nursing stations in a disarray of harried faces and fidgeting bodies, men and women reluctant to meet his gaze, but watching him as he passed them by. He was in shock, he decided. He'd probably been in shock for a long, long time.

The doorway glowed.

She had always liked it bright inside, even when she was sleeping. Clara only grudgingly ever consented to lights being out. The electric bill was just a tax for living, she always said. When they took her in, when it became all too clear that her hospital bed was a destination instead of some brief side trip, she never let the lights go off again.

He stood at the threshold, gazing in upon his queen. His life. His love.

Clara lay in that high bed, sinking down into the pillow, skeletal and frail. She lay there until her breath rattled, until she reached for Norman's hand and he spoke his final, criminal words of comfort. She lay there until she died.

Up on the dais, Kiya sat upon her throne.

CHAPTER
TWENTY-FIVE

She wore a crown with the golden disc of a sun upon her brow. Her body was a blackened husk, flesh polluted by age and bone and poisons of the air. Her nakedness was exposed but for the veil which dangled from her gilded mantle, smeared dull with ancient gore. The veil trembled and swayed with each breath, and beneath it, Norman could see the contours of a blasphemic visage. Too-wide pits where eyes might have been. A jutting, inhuman snout stretched wide with jagged fangs. Hands ended in claws. Feet ended in hooves. Her image reflected the price of her actions.

A wet trail of reddened drool dangled and swayed like a pendulum from behind the veil. It gleamed in the incarnadine light.

"Kiya-Aten," Norman said.

The shrieking in his mind stopped.

Only the awful ragged breathing remained, a counterpoint to the beating of his own heart.

Kiya-Aten.

An absurd wealth of treasures heaped up in every corner and on either side of the throne, of gold and carved precious stone, their purposes used up as the gods to whom they beckoned were destroyed. Shattered urns, cracked altars, scepters snapped in half. Hieroglyphics glowed wetly in the walls, streaked in blood that had trickled down from grates and hidden channels through the ceiling. The glyphs were easy to recognize, her title etched with fury into the stone and filled with the radiance of her hatred.

Besides the living corpse Queen and her treasures, the room was empty except for one final sarcophagus, carved not from precious metals but from woven blocks of ivory. Of bone.

The sarcophagus lay empty, except for a neat stack of wrappings.

He could do this, he assured himself. Just be slow, be patient. Slow was smooth, smooth was fast. If he could get close enough, he might be able to... he wasn't sure. Light her on fire? He wondered if Sieber had a lighter on him, but he knew she would never allow him back out of the corridor. This course, like so many others, only ran one way.

The head pivoted, turned to gaze upon him from behind the veil and he could feel the weight of her attention like an oceanic current. She did not rise from her throne. His hands trembled uncontrollably as he raised them in a placating gesture.

"Don't be afraid," Norman whispered to himself. His voice cracked. He looked for some weapon to use if she sprang toward him, but the futility of the effort brought no comfort. The reddened glow gleamed off a history of treasures that were ultimately useless.

"Don't be afraid," he said again.

"Don't be afraid. It's okay, Clara," he'd told her in that last, awful moment. *"I'm here,"* he said. *"I'm here. I'll always be here."*

And he'd lied.

He'd stayed after she had passed. Until he could no longer kiss her hand good bye with chapped lips, until the room was needed and they draped her in a thin white cloth to push her to the morgue, the summary of the love of his life transformed into a vague silhouette of linen on a comfortless bed.

Then they'd taken her off to some cold metal basement cell and left him to pick up her things, his things, and go home to a house that was a shared promise now broken, full of relics of the two dead inhabitants.

When his feet failed to respond, he gripped the edge of the ivory box to pull himself closer. Felt the writing beneath his fingertips. Not a hackwork of obscenity and violence, like the other glyphs, but simple scholarly writing. Words he had read before, words he didn't even need to see to recognize.

A list of names.

Her husband. Her daughter. Her whole family. Her original family, back in Mitanni, and her new one from Egypt, their names listed one after the next, like a poem of love or of venomous suffering. All dead before her. All prepared and laid to rest while she was left shouting the name of a foreign God who ignored her even as she seethed beneath the sands in His service for endless years. The weight of her countless crimes was nothing compared to the cruelty of her loss.

And above them all, the solitary God, Aten. Undying. Unyielding. Unanswering.

It wasn't her tomb. It was Aten's, prepared and waiting. It was her home.

A wave of bitter sorrow washed over him and took with it his terror. To have served her God relentlessly, and to lose everything just the same. To give her life into an unending service and be ignored, out of reach of sun, out of reach of everything she loved. What blame could he find in the face of such an immortal crime?

The creature on the throne should have held fear for him, but instead he found himself near tears.

What a strange and lonely thing, to live while others died.

"I'm not going to leave you here. Not alone," he told her.

The Lost Queen's hands clenched into a mess of talons and the drool dangled lower, but the rest of her body remained stiff as Norman reached up and slid the mantle from her brow. The tattered veil slipped aside from the cavernous blasphemy of her face. He did not flinch to gaze upon her.

When he lifted her up it was as though he lifted an armful of dried kindling, and he could remember only a winter stretch between semesters, the year before he had married her. Too poor to afford a real trip, they had huddled instead for a week in the false comfort of primitive, self-sufficient glory—a borrowed log cabin, a smoldering hearth, heavy blankets and the warmth of younger skin.

He carried her with the tenderness of a husband carrying his new bride across the threshold of his home.

When he wound the burial dressings around her, he did not rush. He could remember only those first trying years after the devastating news. The hopeful delusion that she would beat this, that helping her into those awful hospital gowns was something temporary, to look back upon with fondness and pride, years later, as they watched their suns set.

And when at last she lay inside her final house of bone, he could remember only the gentle sound of a coffin settling, of gritty dirt thumping down upon a hollow chest wherein lay the only real treasure the world could offer.

Kiya's hand reached out from within and snapped down upon his wrist. Long and filthy claws formed a jagged manacle. Not piercing, but not relenting either.

"Don't be afraid. I'm here, Kiya," he whispered. "I'm here. I'll always be here."

The red light dimmed and extinguished and Norman was as good as his word.